PLAYING NURSIE

Mary Melissa Mercy was dressed in the uniform of a nurse, complete with sensible white shoes and white gloves.

Well, not completely like a nurse.

When the beautiful, flame-haired female uncrossed her legs, Remo could see in the briefest flash she wore nothing under her skirt.

What he couldn't see, however, was what she had under her gloves. Nails that could puncture the flesh as easily as a knife going through butter.

"It appears we have a little time to kill," Mary Melissa said, her words an open invitation.

And she meant exactly what she said, as Remo was about to find out. . . .

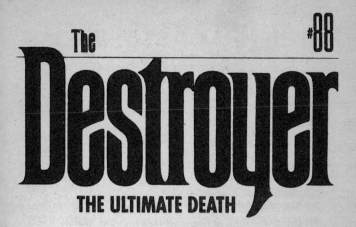

The Destroyer #88

THE ULTIMATE DEATH

CREATED BY

WARREN MURPHY & RICHARD SAPIR

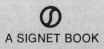

A SIGNET BOOK

SIGNET
Published by the Penguin Group
Penguin Books USA Inc., 375 Hudson Street,
New York, New York 10014, U.S.A.
Penguin Books Ltd, 27 Wrights Lane,
London W8 5TZ, England
Penguin Books Australia Ltd, Ringwood,
Victoria, Australia
Penguin Books Canada Ltd, 10 Alcorn Avenue,
Toronto, Ontario, Canada M4V 3B2
Penguin Books (N.Z.) Ltd, 182–190 Wairau Road,
Auckland 10, New Zealand

Penguin Books Ltd, Registered Offices:
Harmondsworth, Middlesex, England

First published by Signet, an imprint of New American Library,
a division of Penguin Books USA Inc.

First Printing, April, 1992
10 9 8 7 6 5 4 3 2 1

Ⓢ REGISTERED TRADEMARK—MARCA REGISTRADA

PRINTED IN THE UNITED STATES OF AMERICA

PUBLISHER'S NOTE
This is a work of fiction. Names, characters, places, and incidents either
are the product of the author's imagination or are used fictitiously, and
any resemblance to actual persons, living or dead, events, or locales is
entirely coincidental.

For Ric Meyers, Jim Mullaney, Eiríkur Hall-grímsson and our friends at Digital Equipment Corporation—not necessarily in that order.

And for the Glorious House of Sinanju, P.O. Box 2505, Quincy, Massachusetts, 02269. We don't sell books, offer memberships or instruction in the martial arts, but we do read our mail—and sometimes answer it.

1

On the day they suspended his disemboweled body from a tree and drank his salty blood as it bubbled, still warm, from his red, open throat, Gregory Green Gideon was worried about his country's salvation.

There was a terrible irony in this. Gregory Green Gideon believed in health. It was his abiding passion. Yet his unexpected evisceration was destined to enable the greatest menace to the health of the United States since the swine flu to flourish in the very temple Gregory Green Gideon had consecrated to saving America from dietary perdition.

Like most true believers in a great cause, Gideon was not born into his faith, but was a convert to it.

Right up to the very day he quit the Happy Face Ice Cream Company of West Caldwell, New Jersey, to start his own health food concern in the wilds of Woodstock, New York, Gregory Green Gideon had been an unrepentant marketeer of solid sugar frozen foodstuffs. His was a career that blazed across much of the fifties and sixties—the Golden Age of Sugar in American life.

It took his wife's massive coronary to show him the light.

After years of swilling soda and popping bonbons—not to mention slurping down a Happy Face flavorbar after every meal—Dolly Gideon's blood-sugar level was exceeded only by her prodigious weight. She tried diets, starvation, and even a quadruple bypass, but ultimately, her 472 serum cholesterol level brought her down like a blubbery redwood.

Despite her gross looks and grosser eating habits, Gregory G. Gideon had loved his wife. He turned away from her headstone, and then from Happy Face, one dreary autumn day in 1971, and never looked back.

Besides, the handwriting was on the sidewalk. The streets were becoming infested with drug pushers. Parents refused to allow their children to run down the road waving money openly. It was only a matter of time before the jingling neighborhood Good Humor trucks would go the way of the icewagon.

Happy Face ultimately went retail—only to be aced out by gourmet ice creams, which already had their percentage of supermarket space locked up tight. "Confections" and "glaces" with such exotic names as "Hagar Flaven" and "Bordeaux Crême" would supplant mere ice cream—even though they were made in Bethlehem, Pennsylvania.

No, the future lay in health foods, Gregory Green Gideon decided. He tore up his pension, threw away his ties, burned his wing-tips in a potbellied stove, and moved into an environmentally friendly log cabin in New York State. There he was, forty-five, short, paunchy, and balding—the absolute image of the stereotypical salesman as played by any number of middle-aged New York actors—about to embark upon a frightening new sugar-free life, like a pioneer of old.

His years of food sales experience ultimately stood him in good stead. If there was one thing he had learned, it was that people buy food for three reasons. First, to stay alive. But once you got past that, there remained only the two sides of the eternal food coin: because they thought it would taste good, or, more importantly to Gregory G. Gideon, because they thought it was good for them.

Gideon had spent a lifetime convincing the public of the former. Now he was out to convince them of the latter. He started with a single product: a strange fruit-and-nut bar made by Violet Nussbaum, an old woman in neighboring Bethel, New York. She would grind up figs, dates, and mandarin oranges, cement them together with honey, then mix in ground-up chestnuts, pecans, and acorns. She called it the "Mysterious East Bar," and tasting it was like rolling around Yellowstone Park with your mouth open.

Gideon bought the rights to mass-produce the thing for seven hundred and fifty dollars. Within a year the old woman had passed away, and Gregory G. Gideon's "Fru-Nutty Bar" made its fetid debut under the Three-G label.

To say it was an immediate success would be stretching the truth, but like Gideon, the Fru-Nutty Bar had staying power—and a strange, barky aftertaste. He kept pushing, and the public kept tasting.

The new health food manufacturer was amazed. Every fiber in his ice cream-oriented body told him he was committing commercial suicide by mainlining a log of strangled fruit and nuts, but he broke even within a year. Within two, he was making a tiny profit.

Revitalized, Gregory Green Gideon put his marketing skills to work to find out exactly why anyone in his right mind would buy—let alone eat—such a thing.

He commissioned a private poll.

Gideon quickly learned that health faddists don't think food is good for them unless it tastes bad. They liked the Fru-Nutty Bar because it looked, tasted, and was named so ridiculously. It made them feel somehow stronger for having consumed the unconsumable, like brushing their teeth with salt and baking soda.

Gregory followed up his original offering with the new, Vitamin C-enriched Cee-Fru-Nutty, which made them pucker. Then came the new, oat-packed Bran-Fru-Nutty, which made them constipated.

Either way, the customers knew they were getting what they had paid for. Gideon patently refused to make the eating experience more palatable with a chocolate covering or the more fatty nuts, like cashews, and said so right on the label. In fact he eventually took out the honey, and replaced it with a truly revolting soybean paste. It had a nice sheen to it, though.

Word soon got around health food circles that Gregory G. Gideon wasn't fooling anybody. He wasn't selling "lite" products that were actually "hevy." He wasn't hiding lower calories behind higher fat content.

He was giving his public exactly what it wanted. There was no stopping him. The initial snack bars became an entire line of Fru-Nutty supplements: Fru-Nutty Chips snacks, Fru-Nutty

Smoothie drinks, Fru-Nutty All-Grain Burgers, and even bite-sized Fru-Nutty Suckers.

Gideon was stunned by the amount of money that poured in, and he plowed it back into Three-G, Inc. He went from a rented storefront to a run-down factory, then from a ten-year-old warehouse to a brand-spanking-new office and manufacturing building built specifically to his requirements.

Unlike Happy Face Ice Cream, which was housed in a vintage World War II building that would have made Rosie the Riveter nostalgic, the Three-G Incorporated building was all clean, shaded glass, with alternating solar heat panels in a checkerboard design. It was built in the shape of a square, with a small park in the center like a carob-and-pistachio center.

On the last day his blood warmed his own body, Gregory Green Gideon stood before one of the picture windows, contemplating what he had wrought. He stared out at the little grove nestled in the middle of his headquarters, the ultra-modern glass panels shielding the ultraviolet and infrared rays of the sun from his eyes. He watched as the fruit trees and nut bushes swayed in the early morning wind. He smiled tightly at the thought of them taking nutriment from the very ground where his wife and elderly benefactor lay.

"To everything," he hummed, "turn." His loved one had died, to be buried in the earth, to serve as sustenance to the insects—who themselves were crushed into the dirt to feed the foliage. Then the trees and flowers grew fat with fruit, only to fall to the ground and feed the earth once more.

All I do, Gideon reflected on the day of his death, is interrupt the cycle somewhat. I take the fruit of the dirt, grind it up, and feed it to my fellow man.

And they ate it, too. No matter how bad it tasted. But—and this was a big "but"—not, contrary to popular belief, no matter how bad it looked. And therein lay the problem of the day.

"Turn, turn, turn," he muttered, suiting words to action. He now faced the top of the giant silver tureen. He stood on one of the elevated walkways of his manufacturing division. They formed a big square around the edges of the room, then made an X between the four mixing vats that stood twenty feet high in the space.

He stared with a tight frown at the tureen top, his hands behind his back. "There is a season," he sang, taking a jaunty step forward. Between him and the tureen was a small table, upon which was a small plate, upon which was a single portion of the product which was being mixed in the vat at that very moment.

Gregory G. Gideon looked down at what he was promoting as a "Bran-licious Chunk Bar."

"It looks like a cow pat," he complained to his staff. They could only look stunned and stare reproachfully at each other while clutching clipboards. "You call that a Chunk Bar?" he asked, motioning toward it. "We can't call that 'Bran-licious.'" He pinned his top researcher with a stare. "What does that look like to you?" he demanded.

Despite his years of testing products that would make bulimia seem a viable alternate lifestyle, Gideon was still small, rotund, and balding. He had the shape and demeanor of a child's clown punching bag. The kind with the smiling face and round red nose. The kind that, no matter how hard you hit it, rolls back upright with the same pleasant smile.

The researcher lifted his square granny glasses, poked his sharp nose at the flattened, lumpy brown thing on the plate, and sniffed. "It looks," he said dryly, "like a cow pat."

"Exactly," said Gideon. "Exactly. And there's no way we're going to rename this 'Bran Turd.' When I say 'Bran-licious,' I *mean* 'Bran-licious.' "

"What's the difference?" wondered a firm, female voice.

The air conditioning seemed to get cooler, and quieter. An unspoken gasp hung in the air, like a popped soap bubble. The group parted like the Red Sea to reveal Elvira McGlone, the head of marketing.

Gideon had gotten her straight from Manhattan's prestigious University School Of Business. They turned out corporate warriors who were as tight as hemp and as tough as railroad spikes. They produced graduates who could convince the Nazis they lost the war only for lack of effective PR.

McGlone was no exception. And Gideon liked that. Truth be told, he had recruited her because the rest of his staff were retrograde hippies hibernating in Woodstock. She stood out among them like Teddy Kennedy trying to pass himself off as one of the New Kids On The Block.

The entire staff were in lab coats, but beneath those all was jeans and flannel. McGlone was in a tailor-made Lady Brooks suit that might have been stitched around her as she stood fuming impatiently. Her dark blond hair was tied in a bun so severe people swapped unfounded rumors of a face-lift, and her makeup seemed to have been applied by a sharpened tongue-depressor. Her expression might have been chopped from ice. She made the word "sexy" sound like a curse.

"Mr. Gideon," she replied in a condescending tone, "if only you'd let me show you how to position your products in the marketplace."

"I already know our 'position in the marketplace,' " Gideon said testily. "We are the company with the solid product. Not," he stressed, "the hard sell." Then he added, his voice acquiring an edge, "I don't want a new ad campaign, I want a Bran-licious Chunk Bar!"

He stared at them. And they stared back. They stood that way for a full fifteen seconds before Gregory G. Gideon blinked. "Oh, go on. Go on," he said, waving them away. "Get out of here. We'll mix it in yogurt cups and freeze it if we have to."

The others mumbled their full support and shuffled out the side door.

Only McGlone remained behind to try to reason with Gregory Green Gideon.

"If only you'd put in a little more glucose . . ." she began.

Gideon sighed. "Ms. McGlone," he said. "You still don't understand. Our customers don't drink a product simply because the latest singing star is being paid to do so. Our customers don't eat a product just because they see a dozen dancers in leotards singing their hearts out on television. They're the kind of people who read labels. They're the kind of people who notice the word 'glucose,' and its positioning in the ingredients list. And if it's anywhere other than the very, very last, they don't put it in their bodies. And, what's worse for you and me, they don't buy it."

Her face still wasn't registering anything but stiff impatience. He tried one last time—not knowing it was truly the very last time.

"Ms. McGlone—Elvira," he pleaded. "We are not selling cola. We can't take something of no nutritional value and create a sensation through packaging and promotion. We're selling physical well-being here, not peer pressure. We're selling self-control, not self-destruction. Turn your thinking around. I know it tastes bad, but it isn't bad. In fact, if you eat enough of it, it actually begins to taste good."

It was useless. There was a "gone fishing" sign inside the frosty blonde's eyes. She was deep inside her own head, doublechecking her mental market-share.

"Think about it," he said anyway.

"I'll write a report," she replied tightly, and turned away, removing her white jacket in defiance.

Gideon watched her go, eyeing with curious detachment her firm, workout-toned rear beneath the tight, tailor-made skirt. Shaking his bald head, he turned away.

The sun warmed his face, and the garden blew in the upstate breeze. He inhaled deeply, feeling the expensive shirt, knotted silk tie, and tailor-made, three-piece suit give with the breath. No piece of his wardrobe was cheap, or itched. He had money in his pocket and in the bank. He had a solid company, and a future.

Life wasn't bad. No, it wasn't bad at all. If only he could figure out how to make this bran-dung look like a bran bonbon.

Gregory G. Gideon put his hands on the edge of the giant tureen. The stainless steel felt thick and cold to the touch, creating its own strange comfort. He looked down into the lumpy brown mass, and tried to think like a health nut.

What did the mixture require to make it work? Gideon closed his eyes and saw a vision of Fru-Nutty Balls, wrapped in recyclable paper, with the G.G.G. imprint on the flat bottom of every single one. He imagined hands pulling open the paper seams to reveal a crunchy, chunky nugget of fiber, fruit, and pasty nuts, all held together with . . . what?

"Color."

For the first time in years, Gregory G. Gideon began to think in color. There was more to the health food life than pasty white, deep black, sticky brown, or shades of gray. There were blueberries, and yellow corn, and oranges, and ripe red strawberries.

Gregory G. Gideon saw red. Ruby-red apples. Rich red cherries. Rose-red raspberries. He saw a swirl of red curling through the Bran-licious Chunk Bar. He saw the scarlet vein corkscrewing up along the sides of the circular muffin, giving it just a touch of sin and holding it together.

But what should it be? he wondered. Which berry should it be?

"Blood," a raspy voice intoned from somewhere in the room.

Gregory G. Gideon blinked. "What?" he said.

"Blood," the raspy voice repeated.

Gregory Gideon turned around, his hands still on the tureen lip for balance. He found himself staring into the face of the most beautiful girl he had seen since his wedding day.

She was as different from Elvira McGlone as a gem was from a rock. She shamed McGlone's sex. There was absolutely no purpose for McGlone to be a woman as long as this creature existed. Her hair was red—strawberry blond, in fact. Her eyes were green. Her nose long. Her lips curled in a tiny perpetual smile. And freckles danced across her smooth flesh.

She was a vision in white. She was dressed all in white; from the tip of the strange cap nestled in her fiery mane, through her zip-front dress, down her stockinged feet, to the bottom of her sensible white shoes. She was absolutely lovely.

But she was not the one who had spoken. She couldn't be. That voice had been raspy and thin, with a singsong tone. It had ended, even the single word, with a slight sound of complaint that grated on the ear.

"And who might you be?" he wanted to know.

She smiled down on him, a half-foot taller, and not as far away. Her curling lips curled all the more, and she said in a husky whisper, "Mercy."

Gideon was stunned, and enraptured. She was a sensual wild child, as natural as McGlone was packaged. She wore no makeup, but still her eyes shone, her lips were soft and inviting.

All manner of questions came immediately to mind, but what he said was, "What do you want?"

He immediately regretted it. Because that other voice returned, repeating what it had said before.

"Blood."

The beautiful, wild-haired girl with the cosmetics-free face stepped aside, looking over her right shoulder. As she gave way, another figure appeared. Standing in the center of the elevated walkway was a hunched, sunken-cheeked, emaciated Asian man.

He wore a black gown with ornate red piping that went from his chin to the bottom of his sternum. The ends of his sleeves and hem were likewise decorated with intricate red weaving. But that held Gideon's attention only for a fleeting second. What was most interesting was the skeletal man's head.

His hair was thick around the fringe of his skull, although the crown of his scalp was totally bald. The hair was long, coming to his shoulders, and a strange color of steel-blue. His skin tone was dark, and an equally strange color, as if he had a disease.

Gideon remembered that one of his wife's distant relatives had a fluid disorder, which flushed her flesh almost green. This man seemed to have rust inside him, because what once must have been pale, even yellowing, flesh, was now a deep, sickly purple.

His lips were dry, his nose upturned like a pig's, and his almond-shaped eyes covered with the stiffest of skin parchment.

"What did you say?" Gideon asked breathlessly, a sudden tightness in his chest.

"Blood," said the purple Oriental for the fourth time, his lips coming off his yellow-stained teeth, and his eyelids finally rolling up.

The Oriental's pupils were revealed, white as milk. Gregory Gideon could see that the other man could not. He was totally blind.

It was the purple-skinned man's sudden emptiness of expression that inspired Gideon to move. All emotion had left the man, as if a spigot on his throat had opened and any feeling had coursed out of his face and into his torso. He had the dull, dead look of a shark as it sinks its fangs into its prey.

"Missy," the Oriental hissed, and the radiant vision of femininity lifted her left hand.

It seemed the most gentle of movements, as if she were directing a servant where to put her ice tea, but abruptly the girl's hand got between Gideon and the space between the two strangers.

The health food entrepreneur stopped dead in his tracks when he felt her fore-fingernail slip beneath the flesh of his double chin.

He had just glimpsed it as it slid beneath his view. It had been a half-inch long, with no color—only the gleam of some strength-giving polish. Its edge had been cut diagonally in a perfect line, like a guillotine blade.

It was incredibly sharp and thin. So sharp and so thin that it slipped through two layers of his skin without igniting a single nerve ending.

But he knew it was there. He felt it, like a dull pressure. It seemed to spread across his entire body, paralyzing him.

"Hey!" Gregory Green Gideon said in surprise.

"Don't worry," the girl said mildly. "I'm a trained nurse."

Only then did he recognize her wardrobe. She had been too close, and he had been too surprised. It was a nurse's uniform. But now surprise had turned to shock, and she was holding an organic needle at the juncture where his head met his neck.

"*My* nurse," said the strange purple man, now as close to him as she was. "For a quarter-million days, she had nursed me back from life—the life which the *gweilo* with tiger's blood had cursed me to. For five million hours, she toiled to return me to my natural place—amid the Final Death."

Gideon's eyes were like pinballs, bouncing from one of the strangers to the other. He echoed the unfamiliar word. " '*Gweilo*'?"

"Foreign devil," the strawberry-blond goddess translated with a smile. "Devil-man."

Gideon started to protest, but the cuticle in his throat forced him to quiet down. "What," he whispered hoarsely, "are you talking about?"

"You must forgive me," the ancient one said without apology. It was more of an order. "I am an old man, who knows too much of human ways. Although I cannot see I can peer into human souls, and I know what evil lurks there."

Gideon frowned, wondering where he had heard that phrase before. He almost asked, but the implanted fingernail made him think better of it.

"Why me?" he finally asked.

The old Asian's long, thin, drooping eyebrows furrowed. "You must know," he said. "Can't you even perceive it?" His long, wide palm rose smoothly like an ornate kite, his fingernails looking even stronger and sharper than his nurse's. They came to rest lightly on Gideon's vest.

Gideon was surprised by the man's gentle touch, and perfect placement. Although his white eyes were turned away, it was as if the diseased old man could see.

"You are not of the stomach-desecrators," the pale purple Asian said. "Although I can smell the meat you have eaten, you are not one of them."

"One of *who*?" Gideon said quickly, in panic. He looked pleadingly at the young woman, but her expression was as placid as an untroubled pond.

"The stomach is the center," said the old man, lightly rolling a button on Gideon's vest between his middle and fore fingernails. "It is the house of all life and death. The soul dwells there. Destroy the stomach, and you destroy all. It is the death of the Final Death."

There were those words again: "the Final Death." It was not where the old man was coming from. If he could be believed, or even comprehended, it was where he was going.

"We are the holy saviors of the stomach," continued the old man with a sickly, unseeing smile. "We travel the earth as the living dead, punishers of all those who embrace meat."

"Oh, God!" Gideon moaned. A cult, he thought. He had heard of these wild-eyed crazies who lived in the Catskill Mountains, but he had never encountered them.

"No God," the old man intoned. "Only the Final Death." He brought his visage directly in front of Gideon's face. "You had promise," he told the frightened man. "You could have been one of us."

The old man sighed leakily. "But the *gweilo* tiger must be punished. He must know the Final Death. He must become one with it."

He turned his head until his large, delicate left ear was pointing directly at the girl's mouth, his white eyes staring at Gideon. "Do you remember?" the old man asked her.

"Oh, yes," she said with a warm smile, and looked directly at Gregory Green Gideon. "I'm sorry," she told him pleasantly. "You're a nice man." Then she flicked her finger.

All at once, Gregory G. Gideon could hear the sea. He could feel the wind off the desert. And far in the distance, he could see his wife Dolly waving at him. She had never looked more beautiful.

Free of the fingernail in his throat, he stumbled away. His hands slapped the edge of the tureen, and he lurched over the edge. He caught himself just before his feet left the walkway.

Odd, he thought. Someone was whistling. It was an odd whistling. Tuneless. Prolonged. But that wasn't possible, because both strangers were still talking.

"The cutting of the lifeblood," the old man recited.

"The slitting of the throat," the girl answered.

"The release of the life-force," he continued.

"The slicing down the stomach," she replied.

"The destruction of the Holy House," he said.

"The stripping of the carcass," she said.

"The homage."

"The Final Death."

Gregory G. Gideon smiled. His mouth muscles could hardly sustain it, and his lips moved like weak rubber bands, but he smiled. He couldn't help it. The whistling was somehow relaxing. He felt every muscle in his being relax as it continued inexhaustibly. He had never felt anything like it before.

Gregory Green Gideon never knew it was the sound of his life's breath escaping through the paper-thin slice in his throat, before the blood erupted through.

All he knew was that suddenly the whistling was gone, and all his troubles were over. The swirl of scarlet he had been looking for was coursing down the side of the tureen and making a lovely ribbon of red in his Bran-licious Chunk Bar.

After they had skinned the meat from the raw bones, and drank of his blood, the purple-skinned Asian turned his sightless eyes in the direction of the wind. He sniffed the air. Revulsion twisted his corpse-like features.

"Missy," he asked, "what do your eyes see?"

The redhead looked down into a verdant valley, her green eyes narrowing to grow hateful as a cat's. Her lips were now too red.

"I see, Leader, a valley desecrated by a terrible place."

"What kind of a place?"

"It is a place of torment, of slaughter, where people wallow in outrage. Where men profit from unbridled inhumanity."

The old Asian nodded. "And what is the name of this unholy abode?"

"It proclaims itself 'Poulette Farms.'"

The old Asian addressed as "Leader" nodded. "It is there that we will begin," he said, his pig-like nostrils dilating before the scent on the wind, his blank eyes unwinking as a serpent's gaze. "And if our ancestors are with us, it is there that the House of Sinanju will end."

2

His name was Remo, and all he wanted was the popcorn.

"Butter?" asked the bored youth behind the counter.

"That's not butter," said Remo. No one paid any attention to him, since he was wearing black slacks and a black T-shirt. It was warm even at night now, so everybody was wearing T-shirts, jeans, and athletic shoes.

No one paid any attention to his deep-set dark eyes above pronounced cheekbones, or his unusually thick wrists either. Any white man in this neighborhood had better be pumping iron— for his own good.

Of course no one noticed that it was only his wrists which were "ripped"—as if Remo had been doing wrist curls eight hours a day for the last twenty years and no other exercise. Everybody in the theater lobby was an expert in the art of avoiding eye contact.

The bored youth returned to the streaked, cracked-glass counter, and plopped down a cup the size of a small snare drum filled to overflowing with yellow-white kernels, completely coated in a shiny liquid.

"Three dollars," the bored boy said in a bored voice.

The sickly odor of the stuff attacked Remo's nostrils, making him grimace. "No butter," he said.

The boy ignored him, until he realized that his outstretched hand was covered by neither bill nor coin. "Huh?"

"I said, no butter," Remo repeated.

The boy blinked. "Yes, you did."

"No, I didn't. What I said was, 'That's not butter.' "

The boy blinked again. "You said butter," he repeated stubbornly.

" 'Butter' was in the sentence," Remo agreed, "but it was not used in the affirmative."

The boy finally looked directly at him. "Huh?"

"Hey, man!" barked a teenager behind him. "Get your friggin' popcorn and get outta the way!"

Remo looked over his shoulder. A latino teenager in a leather cap with no bill, a baseball jacket, no shirt, plenty of gold chains, ripped denims, and oversized basketball shoes with loose laces stood there, exuding defiance. Remo's even gaze, high cheekbones, and thin lips didn't impress him. His expression of hostile sullenness seemed to have been cast in iron at birth.

"I am trying to purchase popcorn," Remo said. "And it isn't easy."

"He said butter," the counter boy added, as if they were on a TV court show and the tough in the leather cap was the judge.

"That's not butter," Remo said more loudly. "It's flavored soy oil, and has the same effect as coating your stomach with 10W40." He pushed the huge cup back at the boy. "I want *no*—accent on the *no*—butter."

The counter boy looked like he was going to complain again, but he saw no pity in Remo's eyes, and no patience in the tough's. "Okay, okay," he said, dumping the soiled kernels into a plastic garbage can. The only thing that cost money was the cup anyway. He went to scoop out another wad of popcorn.

"No," said Remo. His tone stopped the boy in mid-movement. He looked up in annoyance.

"Not that stuff," Remo said casually. "That's got a monosodium glutamate and salt mixture on it." The boy looked down at the popcorn as if it were poisoned. "The yellow stuff," Remo explained.

"Yellow stuff?"

Remo turned to keep the tough informed. "They pour the stuff onto the kernels while it's popping," he said. "It's supposed to keep it fresh, but all it actually does is make you thirsty, so you'll buy carbonated fructose water, which will make you hungry all over again."

The hood in the leather hat looked him straight in the eye, his jaw jutting out. "You loco, man?"

"No," said Remo. "I used to work in a movie theater when I was a boy. I know this stuff."

What he wasn't telling them was that it had been this very theater where he had worked. As his employer might say: "That wouldn't be prudent." Even if a deep check of employment records couldn't possibly reveal the name Remo Williams. They had been pulled and burned long, long ago. After Remo Williams' death.

The Rialto Theater in Newark, New Jersey, had fallen on hard times since Remo left to become a Newark policeman. It had been shut down the last time Remo had been on lower Broad Street, but some brave businessman had refurbished it just within the last three years.

In that time the tile floors had cracked, the curtains had been ripped, the ceilings had grown dirty, and the lobby video games locked down with more chains than in an Alabama prison, but the remnants of its glory days were still there. No matter how many walls and increasingly smaller screens they installed to make ends meet, the Rialto still held memories.

Remo remembered seeing *Dr. No*, *The Three Stooges in Orbit*, *Psycho*, and *Gorgo* here. He remembered his high school dates clutching at his arm, and how he had clutched at their shoulders, waists, and chests in response. He remembered the cuddling and kisses. But most of all he remembered the huge heroes on the big screen, taking on every kind of villainy and blasting it into eternity without ever losing their hats.

"Take your damn popcorn and get the hell outta my way, man!" snarled the hood.

Remo looked into the teenager's dead, defiant eyes. The tough was practically begging him to try something. He wanted any excuse to blow off the steam of the streets.

It reminded Remo of his other life. He saw it behind his own eyes, as if it were one of the Rialto's movies. He remembered his trial for killing a pusher. He remembered the guilty verdict. He remembered the last meal, the long walk, and the cold strapping-in ritual at the electric chair, as if he had just come from it.

And he remembered the switch being pulled.

He remembered waking up in Rye, New York, at a sanitarium that looked like a cross between a computer factory and a high school. He remembered a tiny old man with wispy white hair and beard who could dodge bullets. He remembered the old Korean teaching him how to do it.

Remo saw in the teenager's eyes the reflection of what he had become. "Here," he said, grabbing the popcorn tub from the counter boy's hands and giving it to the hood. "On me."

The teen stared at him; first in surprise, then in distrust, but finally in grudging acceptance. "Needs butter," he grumbled, thrusting it back across the counter.

Remo leaned on his elbow on the counter. "By all means," he said, gesturing to the counter boy. "Slather on the soybean oil."

As the counter boy worked the antique butter pump, the latino youth sized up Remo. "You queer or something?" he spat.

"You're welcome," Remo said pleasantly.

"Yeah, yeah, *gracias*."

When the transfer was complete and Remo had paid, the hood trudged away and the boy behind the counter heaved a sigh of relief. "Do you know who that was?" he asked.

"No," said Remo. "Who?"

The boy looked at Remo as if he were an alien. Then his expression changed. Remo could see that the boy realized that was what this skinny white man most probably was—to this neighborhood. "Only Tarantula," he said. "Head of the Spanish Spiders, that's all."

Remo glanced after the hood in the hat with mild interest, but the teenager had already gone inside Cinema Three, under the sign that read TRANSFORMED TEEN TAEKWON DO TERRAPINS III: SHELL GAME.

"No kidding?" he grunted to the boy behind

the counter. He leaned forward conspiratorially. "But now that we're alone, let's make a deal. I bet you've got an actual, honest-to-god popcorn-popping machine in the back. How much would it take for you to make me some with nothing on it?"

The boy looked at him with wonder, then greed. "Nothing?"

Remo made a small space between his forefinger and thumb. "Just enough corn oil to pop it," he said. "But no MSG, no salt, no oleo, and no magic yellow powder, okay?" He pulled out a ten-dollar bill.

The counter boy licked his lips. "It's going to taste awfully bland," he warned.

"That's okay," said Remo. "I'm not going to eat it. I'm only going to smell it."

The theater was already a cacophony of people shouting at the screen as Remo chose a row and carefully slid along the back of the seats in the row in front of it, lightly stepping on the sticky cement floor wherever there were no feet. The row's occupants were ready, even eager, to complain, but he gave them no excuse.

Remo sat down, placing the tub in the middle of his lap. He looked up at the screen. On the billowing, patched white sheet was the blurry image of four humanoid sea turtles in polyurethane and foam-rubber suits. The scene shifted to Central Park at night. It looked just like Central Park by moonlight—except for the ninjas in the trees. They were more plentiful than the squirrels.

Remo held the tub beneath his nose and took a big sniff.

"Ah, that's good!" he breathed, taking another long inhalation of popcorn aroma.

"Whatchu doin', man?" laughed a teenager beside him. "Think that stuff's coke, or something?" He turned to the man beside him, "Hey, Gomez!" he cackled. "Look at the anglo, man! He think the popcorn is some good blow!"

"You wouldn't believe what they put on it nowadays," Remo told him flatly. "It'll burn out your insides."

The boy laughed. "You're flyin', all right." He turned back to the screen. "Bitch is gonna get stuck now!" he shouted.

Remo looked up. Sure enough, the sea turtles' very human and very blond sweet young girlfriend had been surrounded by ninjas near the Alice in Wonderland statue. Just another night in Central Park.

"The bitch'll have to show them where to put it!" a raucous voice shouted. The entire house laughed. Except Remo.

"You don't mean they're going to soil that girl's virtue, do you?" Remo asked in a loud voice, his tone mock-concerned.

A voice laughed. "No man, they wanna pork her! Oink, oink, oink!"

"Imagine that. . . ."

Sure enough, just after the sweet young girl's shirt had been ripped a lone sea turtle showed up, and now the ninjas were circling him. Remo watched in a detached manner, wishing he could actually eat his popcorn.

But his system was now too sensitive to suffer the sharp edges of the puffed kernels. Almost nothing but steamed rice and duck and fish had passed his lips for the last twenty years. He felt sad. What good was it to be the greatest assassin on earth, if he couldn't even eat a simple staple like popcorn?

Cancel that: the second greatest assassin on earth. He was the latest in the unbroken line of Masters of Sinanju. A small, thin, wizened Korean was the keeper of the sun source of all martial artistry. It was this man, the Reigning Master of Sinanju, who had taken the fresh-from-the-grave Remo Williams and taught him proper breathing, correct diet, and more importantly, how to fully utilize the incredible powers locked in his sleeping mind and body so that he could become the enforcement arm for CURE, a government organization so secret only the President knew it existed.

Remo watched. The terrapin—Remo thought he was Porthos—was systematically being pummeled to the ground by ninja nunchuks. But before they could deliver the killing blow, Aramis, Athos, and d'Artagnan popped up from a manhole cover and sent the ninjas flying in all directions.

To Remo's eyes, it looked painfully slow and staged.

The audience went crazy; laughing and hooting and throwing things. A butterfly knife sailed up at the screen and impaled the blonde neatly in her cleavage.

Remo sighed. It hadn't been this much of a zoo when he was young.

His gaze settled on a man in the front row, over on the right aisle, and his face froze. It was Tarantula, reputed head of the Spanish Spiders, and he was taking advantage of the din to tell someone across the aisle what he thought of him.

The object of his abuse was watching the screen intently, but his body was twisted in the

seat toward Tarantula, and there were at least a
dozen teens on either side of the aisle who were
intently interested in his response to the verbal
abuse.

Remo exhaled slowly through his nose.

So much for an evening lost in popcorn aroma
and nostalgia. Taking the tub of popped corn
with him, Remo started to move sideways down
the row. He slid easily across the sticky cement,
as if the soles of his Italian loafers had been im-
pregnated with anti-stick.

". . . you *marachita*," Tarantula finished, snapping his head sideways as if in punctuation.
Then he leaned back, having vented his rage, and
waited for Faroom, Supreme Sheik of Allah's
Swarm, to respond. His posse lounged around
him on the Spanish Spiders' side of the cinema,
their leers mocking, and their attitudes saying
that Faroom couldn't possibly match their leader's invective.

But their smiles disappeared as Dum-Dum
Dudley, the teen beside Faroom, started spitting
a bass beat, and Faroom himself began spewing
an obviously prepared rap.

Obvious, because it was so tight. There was no
way anyone could do that off the top of his head.
The words were coarse, and the rhymes vicious.
They told Tarantula what he could do, where he
could do it, and with whom.

Tarantula's face became an onyx sculpture,
and his baseball jacket billowed open. His fingers
reached quickly inside, and his hand yawned
open to grip the shining, nickel-plated handle of
the weapon within the tan leather shoulder
holster.

Remo flicked a kernel of popcorn in the
tough's direction.

"Snack?" he asked, simultaneously shoving the cardboard tub under Tarantula's nose.

Tarantula's hand came out of his jacket as if his namesake had bitten it, and stared dumbstruck at the crushed popcorn petal imbedded like shrapnel in his hand. He looked to his right just as his main man seemed to vault up in midair back first, then land in the lap of another thug in the row behind him.

Suddenly Remo was sitting beside him, rooting around in the popcorn, intent on the screen. "The movie's pretty lousy," he remarked. "But the floor show's good."

Tarantula looked at Remo, who added, "I see you've finished your popcorn. Care to try some of mine?"

The Spanish Spiders started to rise from their seats, but Tarantula held up his bleeding hand. "You better haul butt out of here, you anglo fruit," he spat.

Remo just kept taking fistfuls of popcorn, looking at them sadly, and dropping them on the floor. "It's a pity," he said. "You can't even go out to the movies anymore."

"Whatchu talkin' about, man?"

"Oh, you know what I'm talking about, Tyrant. May I call you Tyrant?"

"The name's Tarantula, jack-off," the teenager spat at him.

"The name's Remo, Tyrant. I don't suppose you've ever heard of me? I used to be a big name in these parts."

"You're nuts, you know that, man?"

"No, but I am ticked off," Remo said casually, dropping more popcorn. "You want to know why? I'll tell you why. Because I love this place. This is the place where I learned what heroes

are all about. They gave me hope, and made me
want to make the world better."

Remo took a fistful of popcorn. "Then you and
your buddies come along and turn the place into
a shooting gallery. Bad enough you do it on the
streets—my streets—but at least you know where
each other live. Here, you outnumber the innocent bystanders ten-to-one."

He squeezed his fist, and the popcorn turned
to glittering powder. He let it stream out of his
hand. "Now nobody comes to the movies anymore. They stay home, cowering in their living
rooms, watching videos. You're killing movies.
You know what that means?"

The gang made a move toward him, but Tarantula stopped them again. "No, anglo. What's it
mean?"

Remo looked at him and smiled like a skull,
rolling a popcorn kernel on his thumbnail with
his forefinger. "It means that when this genera-
tion grows up, there'll be less people like me,
and more people like you. And that pisses the
hell out of me."

Tarantula gave him his biggest death's-head
smile—the kind that doesn't involve the eyes.
"Well, don't you worry about it, baby." He
quickly reached into his jacket. "Because you're
a dead man!"

Remo let him pull out the gun. He let the others reach for theirs. Then he flicked the single
popcorn kernel on this thumb into Tarantula's
right eye.

The piece of popcorn shot across the small distance like a barbed-wire BB pellet, and had the
same effect.

The popped edges of the kernel tore open Tarantula's pupil, and the corn heart wedged deep

in his cornea. He screamed, as Remo lightly gripped the thick rectangular barrel of the huge automatic weapon.

"That a custom job?" he said lightly. "Looks it. I don't know much about guns. They dilute the art."

Tarantula was in no mood to answer. He continued to scream and turn, one hand over his eye, trying to keep the blood and ocular fluid in. To the others, it looked as if he and Remo were dancing around an invisible maypole.

"Fifteen rounds," Remo judged, examining the weapon. "Nickel-plated. Must've set you back a ton of crack."

Tarantula fixed him with his good eye, brought the gun down until it was against Remo's nose, and pulled the trigger.

Tarantula's right-hand man went down, a smoking crater in his chest. Which was weird, since he stood off to the left.

"Smart move," said Remo, as the rest of the audience started to scream and bolt. "Can't shoot people in the head around here. Skull shrapnel really flies."

Tarantula screamed again. His arm had somehow been moved so it was pointing off to his left. He brought it around until it was against Remo's right breast, and pulled the trigger again.

Something propelled it away. Something too fast to be seen.

Dum-Dum Dudley, coincidentally named for the kind of bullet that killed him, went down next to Faroom.

Ignoring the stampeding audience, the Spanish Spiders and Allah's Swarm all took out their guns—with Remo and Tarantula in the middle.

Tarantula hit the carpet and rolled for his life.

The two street gangs started firing at each other. Normally they'd all miss, hitting a variety of innocent bystanders, but this time they had Remo to contend with. What their bullets didn't accomplish, his hands did.

He weaved among them, pushing and pulling gang members so that ripping lead smashed between ribs and into hearts. He spun, knocking them into the line of fire, jerking their wrists and guns so that their own shots found their marks.

It was like a macabre ballet. Remo was a blur, always one step ahead of death, and although the seats and floor became spattered with blood drops he remained unsprinkled by gore.

Finally the crackle of gunfire abated, and there was no one left but Faroom and Tarantula, who stood on the opposite sides of the wide aisle staring at each other in stunned silence. Remo leaned against the stage. He watched the two gang leaders impassively as the film continued to roll.

The theater was empty, save for those two, and the dozen corpses at their feet. Remo picked up his blood-splattered popcorn tub and began crushing the last of the kernels.

"Play nice," he instructed the gang lords.

They immediately raised their guns like duelists, aimed at each other's faces, and pulled the triggers.

The guns boomed and bucked in their hands. Tarantula's bullet went wide and slammed into an emergency exit's steel latch-bar. It whined away with a grinding snap. Faroom's round cut a chunk out of the stage next to Remo's elbow.

"I said *nice*," said Remo, and flicked a popcorn kernel into Faroom's eye.

As the other gang leader was cycloped he screamed, firing off another round into the ceiling.

Both gang leaders looked at each other through their one good eye, each holding their free hand over their destroyed ones. They were both hunched over, both gasping for breath, and both got the same idea at the same time.

Faroom aimed at Remo. Tarantula aimed at Remo. They transferred their hate for each other to this amazing white man. They pulled their respective triggers and held them down, so that all the remaining bullets in their fifteen-round clips were pumped out. Too late.

Both men danced and jerked as the projectiles ripped into them.

Faroom was perforated from his forehead to his crotch. Tarantula got ten rounds directly in the head, all but blotting out his two-ounce brain.

Remo watched Tarantula crumple to the floor, a big smoking hole in his head. "He who lives by popcorn," he intoned by way of eulogy, "dies by popcorn."

And he walked out into the warmth of the Newark, New Jersey, afternoon.

It was not the Newark he had grown up in. Not the Newark of the orphan Remo Williams, ward of the state, who had left St. Theresa's Orphanage—now a parking lot—for the Newark Police Department, pulled a tour in Nam, and returned to the force only to be framed for the murder of a pusher in the Ironbound section of town.

He had not killed the man, but the state saw it differently. Remo had gone to the electric chair thinking he was about to die.

After the juice had caused him to black out, Remo woke up in the place called Folcroft Sanitarium and discovered that the frame-up had been engineered to erase him so a government agency known as CURE could have its own White House-sanctioned assassin.

Remo Williams.

They had taken away his last name. They had erected a tombstone with his name chiseled in marble. They had destroyed every record with his name, face, and fingerprints on it.

And most cruel of all, they had subjected him to plastic surgery, so that when Remo awoke to the chill unexpectedness of still walking the earth, his own reflection was unsettling and alien.

Over the years Remo had had his face fixed several times, each time getting further and further away from the face that was genetically his own.

But now, over twenty years after it had all begun, Remo walked the streets of his childhood with his original features.

He reveled in the knowledge that if Dr. Harold W. Smith, his superior, were even to suspect he had ventured back to his childhood haunts, he would stroke out. But twenty years was twenty years. Newark had changed. There was no one to remember even the true face of Remo Williams. He would tell Smith that, and that would be the end of any talk of going under the knife again. He hoped.

Remo found himself in the Ironbound section of the city. It had not changed so much. He paused before the alley where the pusher had been found, Remo's badge gleaming in his drying blood.

The place where Remo Williams' life had taken the wrongest turn possible was no shrine. It stank of urine and maggots and rancid leftovers. Remo tried to remember the pusher's name. It wouldn't come. There was a time, when he was imprisoned up at Trenton, when those kinds of unanswered questions had kept him awake at night.

Now Remo Williams no longer cared.

So long ago . . .

He found his car—it was registered to "Remo Meyers," another in a string of disposable aliases—and drove north.

As he drove, he thought back on the events that had given him his old face.

It was hard to tell where it had all begun. Was it Palm Springs? Or Abominadad, Irait? Or Folcroft Sanitarium, where the surgery he had been tricked into undergoing had taken place?

On reflection, Remo decided it all tied together. If it had not been for Palm Springs, where Remo and his mentor had found themselves playing button-button with a live neutron bomb, he would not have ended up in Irait, a tool of the government that had triggered the Gulf War. And if he had not become the official assassin to Irait, his face would not have been broadcast to the world, making it public and forcing Harold Smith to resort to plastic surgery.

The joke had been on Smith, and on the Master of Sinanju.

The plastic surgeon had discovered that Remo's face had been pared down almost to the naked bone. So he had gone in the opposite direction, building up the nose, the chin, the modeling.

And inadvertently, restoring Remo Williams'

original face with nearly one-hundred-percent faithfulness.

Smith had been furious. The Master of Sinanju had been aghast. He had attempted to cajole the surgeon into giving Remo Korean features—Remo still wasn't certain his eyes hadn't been given a slight elongation. No one seemed to agree on this point.

Still, for all Remo's pleasure, there had been a downside. He and Chiun had been forced to vacate their private home, to return to the old cycle of switching residences often.

This time they were in a tower condominium complex on the former site of another landmark of Remo's lost childhood, Palisades Park in Edgewater, New Jersey.

It was there that Remo had left his Master. It was to there he was returning.

Since they had moved, Chiun had lapsed back into his mood of pique, blaming Remo for the fact that the Master of Sinanju had spent three months in a virtual coma at the bottom of a desert structure, where Chiun had taken refuge to escape the exploding neutron bomb.

Three months in which Remo had believed his Master dead. Three months in which Chiun had slept in a watery grave, his spirit appearing before Remo, pleading and attempting to communicate his desperate plight.

And during those three months the Master of Sinanju had hibernated through his one-hundredth birthday, a milestone called the *kohi*.

Chiun had been bewailing that missed moment of glory ever since. And blaming Remo for it.

Remo decided that he had had enough of the missed birthday. Screw the date. Chiun's hundredth-and-first wasn't far off. They'd have a celebration, regardless. Maybe it would get Chiun off his back once and for all.

On the way home, Remo stopped in at a Japanese supermarket to buy a whole duck.

He selected an *oxymura jaimaicensis*, better known as ruddy duck, because it was the most succulent, taking care to select a bird with the least subcutaneous fat content. A lifetime of alternating between duck and fish had made Remo, of necessity, an expert on both species.

Whistling, he grabbed a pound of the kind of Japonica rice that had the nutty aftertaste Chiun liked so much.

Yeah, he thought happily as he stepped out into the cool air that smelled of the nearby Hudson River, this will bring Chiun out of his snotty mood.

3

The thirty-seventh annual Cahill picnic was memorable, to say the least.

They held it, as always, in the back lot of the Fairfax, Virginia, high school, on the sunniest day of the spring. Back when they started the tradition in '55, the extended Cahill family struggled to predict the sunniest day of the season with the help of almanacs, psychics, palm readers, and astrologers. But soon they discovered that the less they tried, the sunnier it was. Old Mother Cahill started to take for granted the fact that the day she chose for the reunion-picnic-barbecue would be the sunniest day of the year.

And while it wasn't always a perfect blue, never had a drop of rain disturbed so much as a single lock of hair on any Cahill head during the annual reunions, or turned any of their paper plates into soggy cardboard leaves.

They came from all over the South, hauling their pots of picnic necessities and vats of regional delicacies. Ted and Cathy Cahill came all the way from New Orleans with their tongue-searing jambalaya. Jack and Ellen Cahill came from Baltimore with red pepper-steamed hard-shell crabs. Don and Chris Cahill came from Sarasota with their onion flowers—whole sweet onions cut into the shape of roses, deep-fried, and tasting like an apple made entirely of onion rings.

But no matter how many culinary heights they scaled, the single favorite item at every one of the thirty-six prior celebrations had always been Old Mother Cahill's fried chicken. That's what got the family to the first reunion, right after Uncle Dan came back from Korea, and that's what brought them back year after year. For more than three decades it had been the first thing they bit into and the last thing they talked about.

This season was no exception. Fluffy white clouds dotted the deep blue sky, the cars filled the faculty parking lot, and the field was covered with a volleyball net, a croquet set, a kickball pole, and a badminton court; but all the relatives came to Old Mother Cahill's table first—to sink their teeth into a crispy, juicy, flaky, light, delicious piece of fried chicken. The party couldn't officially begin until everybody had coated their palates with chicken juice.

The reunion went on all day, as each group of siblings took their turns at the different sporting events, alternating that with more eating. Following the chicken came the festival of salads. There was garden, Caesar, chef's, macaroni, three-bean, Waldorf, egg, tuna, potato, German potato, potato with egg, potato with egg and onion, potato with egg, onion, and celery, potato with egg, onion, celery, and peppers—and chicken.

Then came the main dishes and casseroles, followed by the desserts. They were as myriad and ornate as the salads. There was chocolate layer cake, German chocolate cake, walnut cake, whiskey cake, lemon cake, and linzer torte. There was coconut custard pie, Boston cream, banana cream, and chocolate cream. There was blueberry, cherry, apple, pineapple, mince, pecan, and lemon meringue pie. There were brownies, blondies, cookies, homemade doughnuts, and fried dough. There were even candies and ice cream.

Was it any wonder that at about six o'clock Ted Cahill was feeling a trifle queasy?

He didn't worry. It was expected in the Cahill family. It wasn't until he was twenty-five that he'd realized the burning sensation in his chest wasn't supposed to be there. And by then he had discovered the wonders of beer. His home town of New Orleans had more kinds and more of it than almost anywhere—with the possible exception of Bavaria.

Even so, he saved his serious eating and drinking for the annual reunion. So a certain queasiness was to be expected. He'd just play another game of volleyball to help his digestion, and eventually the feeling would pass.

He joined the crowd around the net, to the hoots and hollers of encouragement from the others. As soon as he took his place in the back row of the players, he was glad he'd made this decision. Directly opposite him, in the back row on the other side of the net, was Milly LeClare, his second cousin on his aunt's side.

Milly just got more beautiful with every passing year. She had to be eighteen now, but she looked at least twenty-one. Her hair was light and loose, her face unblemished and alive, her body firm and shapely. Best of all, she was unconcerned with how the others reacted to her. It didn't affect her naturalness in the least. She played and laughed without concern.

She wore cutoff denim shorts, sneakers, and a loose white shirt. Every time she jumped, her upper body moved in a most exciting way. Whenever the volleyball wasn't near him, Ted watched with interest. Then, every time a side lost a point, he'd watch as the players shifted to their new positions and shouted in unison, "Rotate!"

It was what the move was called, and they'd all shouted it whenever they played, from grammar school on. Milly's side lost a point, and they shifted. Ted's side lost a point, and he shifted parallel to her. Milly's side lost another point, then Ted's side again. Ted lost two in a row, pulling him farther and farther away from the object of his attention, but he played extra hard until Milly's side lost two more.

Each side made more points, and then Ted and Milly were facing each other from just the other side of the net. "Hi, Milly," he said.

She looked back, her eyes sparkling. "Hi, Ted." Her voice was husky from effort. He stared at her a second more, and her eyes smoldered before she lowered her head. Then the ball was served from his side of the net.

Everyone tensed as it bounced from hand to fist to hand. Then it came to Milly. She leaped up, her shirt rising to reveal her flat, smooth stomach, and tried to spike the ball straight down over the net. But Ted was up, his arms raised, and he batted the ball just as it came off her hand.

It spun to the side, practically rolling along the top of the net, as their fingers touched. They both felt an electric shock between them, and were distracted from the game.

Ted landed heavily on his feet, his eyes wide and staring into hers as she landed nimbly. The volley ball continued to fly over their heads as they looked deep into each other's eyes. Something had passed between them, something more than static.

She had always known he liked her, and she was attracted to him for reasons she couldn't begin to understand. Maybe it was chemical, or hormonal, but for whatever reason she had been fascinated by him from the moment they had met years ago.

But now she was of legal age. Now, it didn't matter to her if he was married and had kids. Now she could pursue her interest without being defined as "jailbait." And she knew he was interested in her, too. No matter what happened, at least he couldn't be threatened with arrest. Divorce, yes. Arrest, no.

She idly opened her next shirt button, as if it were too hot.

Then, when the volley ball hit the ground, she took advantage of the teams' jostling and banter to lean over, giving Ted a nice view. For his part he seemed mesmerized, his expression one of incredulous disbelief.

"So," she said breathily. "What are you doing after the game?"

It was like a dream come true for Ted Cahill.

He opened his mouth to answer—and threw up on her chest.

And Ted Cahill was only the first.

Little Johnny Cahill disgorged on the kickball, splattering his aunts and uncles as it spun around the pole. Alicia Cahill vomited on her badminton racket. Little Mickey Cahill puked into the Jell-O molds.

And then the Cahill family started dropping.

Doris Cahill's legs slipped out from beneath her and she cracked the back of her head on a freshly painted picnic table, spilling her husband Neil's beer. Neil would have been more upset about the beer than his wife, had he not collapsed a moment before near their Gatorade-filled cooler.

Old Mother Cahill careened face-first into her portable deep-frier, and began to sizzle.

Milly LeClare landed squarely atop Ted Cahill beneath the volleyball net, one breast sliding free of her loose-fitting T-shirt onto Ted's shoulder.

But Ted couldn't enjoy it. Like Milly and the other Cahills, his tongue had sprouted, bloated and white, from his slack mouth, and his vacant eyes stared heavenward.

All around the field the Cahills got sick, en masse. In fact, everyone who had eaten some of Old Mother Cahill's chicken succumbed to a fast, powerful, deadly food poisoning.

The few Cahills left standing sobbed and screamed and pushed at the lifeless corpses of loved ones.

The sour stench of stomach acid wafted up into the crisp spring air.

Then it started to rain.

Bob Harrison had found himself while he was still in high school.

He had been kidded mercilessly by the other kids at Exeter (New Hampshire) High since that first day when he had strapped on the red and white-striped apron and placed the red ball cap with the golden TBC logo on the front on his

greasy black hair, and assumed his first and ultimate position in life—that of a counter boy.

The kidding had always come down to one
thing.

"Hey, Bob! What's the major's super-secret
recipe?"

Back in those days Americans were a lot less
health-conscious, and so Major Scandills,
founder of TBC, had loaded his famous barbecued chicken with more preservatives than the
ancient Egyptians used on their deceased
pharaohs.

Times had changed, though. Old Major Scandills passed away. The large company was taken
over by eager young executives, who began testing alternatives to the overly spicy super secret
recipe. Even the name of the restaurant chain,
Tennessee Barbecued Chicken, had been up-
dated and shortened to TBC, as if to avoid the
entire cholesterol controversy.

But Bob Harrison still hovered behind the
counter. One constant in an ever-changing
universe.

Truth was, Bob had neither the intelligence
nor the ambition to move any farther up TBC's
chain of command. He became a counter boy the
day he was hired, and he remained a counter boy
to the day he died.

On that latter day, Bob was dragging a soppy
rag across the immaculate counter top when he
noticed someone grazing in the "all-you-can-eat"
salad bar. That was the only way to describe
what the woman was doing. She had her face
planted firmly in the bucket of croutons, and her
hands were hanging limply at her sides. Bob noticed an upended plate of lettuce and carrot

shavings dumped near the woman's motionless feet.

That was too much! TBC had rules. The board of health had made them put sneeze-guards around the salad bar area, so they were certain to frown on people actually putting their faces in the food.

Bob was just about to go out on the floor and wield some of his awesome counter-boy authority when he saw another patron out in the restaurant area vomiting on his formica table top. A split-second later, the same customer clutched at his throat and slid to the mock-brick linoleum floor.

This was too much for Bob. They had opened the doors of the Exeter TBC not half an hour before, so the only people working were Bob, the cook, and the manager. He was certain that neither the cook nor the manager would clean up the mess.

Bob was about to go over and complain to the man beneath the table when another patron vomited, then another. These customers, too, dropped to the shiny floor.

A sudden, horrible thought occurred to Bob Harrison: What if there's something wrong with the chicken? But that couldn't be—he had filched a piece from the kitchen not ten minutes before and he was feeling just fine, thank you.

Bob managed only one step further before a lump of bile and stomach acid launched up his esophagus and splattered the photo of Major Scandills, a memorial that hung in perpetuity in the foyer of all TBC restaurants. The Major didn't seem to mind. Nor did Bob Harrison. His white, distended tongue was pressed lifelessly against the red linoleum floor, held down by his inert head.

In every TBC from Lubec, Maine, to Miami, Florida, the scene was playing out exactly the same. The contagion spread as far west as Dayton, Ohio.

On Wall Street, Tennessee Barbecued Chicken dropped two hundred points, suffering its worst financial setback since the outbreak of the jogging epidemic in the late 1970s.

Harold W. Smith, head of the super-secret government agency CURE, was faced with one of the minor annoyances that plagued what he had tried to make a well-ordered life.

"The cafeteria was out of prune whip yogurt, Dr. Smith."

Eileen Mikulka stood nervously before the broad oaken desk of her employer. She held a steaming styrofoam cup in her slightly plump hands.

As Smith's secretary, Mrs. Mikulka handled the day-to-day operations of Folcroft Sanitarium, freeing up Smith's time so that he could better monitor national and international situations via the massive computers in the basement of the institution. Smith did this by staring almost unblinkingly at the scrolling computer screen, which was now hidden in a secret compartment below the surface of his desk.

Of course, Mrs. Mikulka didn't know this. She believed that Folcroft was just a sanitarium catering to special medical cases.

She only took on the additional responsibility to help out the poor, beleaguered Smith. She took great pride in the way she relieved some of the difficulties in the work life of her perennially harried employer. Dr. Smith always looked as if he were about to collapse under some great personal burden, although for the life of her she didn't know where all that stress could come from. Actually, Folcroft was a rather sleepy place.

"It was all my fault," she confessed. "I should have doublechecked with Mrs. Redlund in the cafeteria. But she's usually very efficient. She told me the truck driver didn't deliver it with the rest of today's order."

Smith waved a dismissive hand. "Quite all right," he said absently, his patrician face registering disapproval. His head was bowed over a sheaf of papers, and an exquisitely sharpened pencil hovered in one hand. He wore a three-piece suit, whose gray fabric nearly matched his hair and skin tones. He adjusted the rimless glasses that were beginning their long slide down and off the bridge of his nose.

"I did get you some soup," she added hopefully. She held the styrofoam container aloft. "Chicken. I thought you might like it instead."

"That will be fine, Mrs. Mikulka."

Carefully, so as not to further disturb her employer, she placed the container on his desk and turned to leave the room.

Smith looked up. "Mrs. Mikulka?"

"Yes, Dr. Smith?" she asked, her hand resting on the doorknob.

"Did you make certain that the sanitarium wasn't billed for the yogurt that did not come in?"

"Of course, Dr. Smith."

"Very good. Carry on."

The moment the door had closed, Harold W. Smith set aside the discharge papers he had been feigning interest in and touched a concealed stud under the rim of his scarred oak desk.

A concealed computer terminal hummed up into view. Smith attacked the unfolding keyboard like a mad concert pianist.

He was once more the director of CURE.

4

The Master of Sinanju was fixated on the big-screen television when Remo entered their condominium apartment.

"I'm home," said Remo, feeling the emptiness of his words echo hollowly. This was not home. This would never be home.

Chiun did not look up from the TV, and its toiling VCR. The Master of Sinanju was enraptured by the slow talkiness of a British soap opera. These were his latest passion. And he was still catching up on the episodes he had missed during his extended coma sleep.

"I said, 'I'm home,'" Remo repeated, light-voiced.

Abruptly, the Master of Sinanju cupped his hands over his delicate ears. Not so tightly that they blocked out the dialogue rolling from the TV speaker. Just enough to deflect other annoying sound waves. Such as Remo's voice.

Remo could tell this by the loose way Chiun's long-nailed birdclaw hands were held.

He shrugged, sighed, and carried his bundle into the kitchen, saying, "We're having duck tonight."

This actually elicited a response from the wispy figure in the silver-and-blue kimono.

"We had duck last night," said Chiun, his voice managing to be squeaky and querulous at once. The overhead light made his head—bald except for two white puffs over each ear—shine like an amber egg.

"Cape Sheldrake," Remo countered.

"I am in no mood for Cape Sheldrake," said Chiun.

"Good. Because that's not the kind of duck we're having."

Out of the corner of his eye, Remo could see the wispy beard that clung to his mentor's tiny chin quiver like a smoky antenna.

Remo stopped. "Well?"

"Well, what?"

"Aren't you going to ask?"

Chiun's tiny, wrinkled face puckered. "No."

"Why not?"

"Because I know it is not ruddy duck. And ruddy duck is the only species of duck that would interest me."

"How do you know it's not ruddy duck?"

The tiny mouth opened, as if to speak.

"I said," Remo repeated, "how do you know it's not ruddy duck, served with that Japonica rice you like so much?"

"Because ruddy duck is not to be found in this barbarian land."

"Could be imported."

"Unlikely," Chiun sniffed, his hands returning to his ears.

"Suit yourself," Remo said casually. He let his grin go wide as he disappeared into the kitchen and got down to cooking.

He had Chiun's interest now. The worst was

over. The ice had been cracked. It was just a matter of time now before the silent treatment would be a thing of the past.

Remo boiled water in the stainless-steel pot. The duck went into the oven.

It began smoking almost at once. The tangy scent of the smoke was unmistakable, and would surely catch Chiun's interest.

Remo kept his eye on the half-open kitchen door as he pulled the succulent duck from the oven and blew the exuding fat from its darkening skin. He half expected to see Chiun poke his inquisitive bald head in at any moment.

But the Master of Sinanju did not.

Remo kept at it. Just a matter of time now. Chiun would have his *kohi*. It would be the best *kohi* he ever could have imagined.

And best of all, Remo wouldn't have to listen to the carping complaints of how he, a mere white, had allowed Chiun to languish under the sands outside Palm Springs, immersed in cold, brackish water, beseeching the gods for release, while Remo wasted his time mourning for one who was not even dead. No longer would Remo have to endure the complaints that he had only pretended ignorance of Chiun's true fate so that he could assume mastership of the House of Sinanju, the finest house of assassins in human history, the house Chiun headed. The house Remo, his adopted son, was destined to assume one dark day when the Master of Sinanju was no more.

Remo set a simple but elegant table, with cherry-wood chopsticks placed carefully beside bamboo plates and bowls. The water was pure spring water, entirely free of chemicals or carbonation.

All that was missing was a birthday cake. Remo had considered doing something with a rice cake, but decided that Chiun's age was still too sensitive an issue to raise just yet. Not while he was stubbornly insisting he was still only eighty.

When the rice was nice and sticky, Remo drained off the water through a bamboo colander and spooned two nearly perfect steaming balls into the proper eating bowls.

Only then did he remove the duck from the oven and place it on a platter in the center of the table. It smelled like ... duck. But it was the kind that Chiun always seemed to crave most, when Remo had returned from food shopping and invariably failed to bring home the coveted species.

Remo removed his chef's apron and stuck his head into the living room.

"Soup's on!" he called cheerfully. Chiun was going to melt like a midsummer's ice cream cone when he saw the spread. It was all Remo could do to hold back a grin of culinary triumph.

Chiun continued to be absorbed in the day-to-day travails of the British gentry. Slowly, he gathered the silvery folds of his evening kimono about his spindly legs.

"It's getting cold," Remo warned. "The rice will lose that rare nutty flavor if you keep it waiting."

Still no response.

Remo was hovering in the half-open door. He eased it open farther and started fanning the succulent scent of roast duckling into the parlor. It would spoil the surprise, but it might produce a reaction.

It did. The Master of Sinanju's severe profile

lifted, like a cat reacting to the scent of prey. His tiny nose sniffed the air, at first delicately, then curiously.

A strange expression came over his features.

Like a gaudy Oriental tent being thrown up on short poles, the kimono-clad form of the Master of Sinanju rose to its full magnificent five-foot height. The bald head, decorated with shimmery fogwisps over each precious ear, swiveled in Remo's direction.

Remo took that as his cue. He threw the door open wide, stepping aside so that Chiun could pass.

Tucking his tiny hands into the closing sleeves of his kimono, Chiun did just that.

Soundless, but with a force like that of a steamship plowing along, Chiun pushed past Remo and entered the kitchen, his face unreadable, but the quiet power of his presence making the exposed hairs on Remo's forearms lift as if from static electricity.

Remo let the door swing closed and followed his mentor in.

Chiun stood dead-still before the spread table. He sniffed here and there. Remo maneuvered to get a good look at his face in profile. The hazel eyes, clear as agates, gleamed with an odd light.

Remo waited for the webbing of wrinkles covering his face to smooth with surprise and appreciation.

Instead, they contracted like a wind-troubled orb web. His tiny nostrils stopped drawing in duck aroma, and the Master of Sinanju straightened like the main sail on a junk.

Just before Remo could get out the words "Not bad, huh?", Chiun asked a question in a level but vaguely indignant voice.

"Why are you trying to poison me?"

"Poison?"

"This duck is poisoned," Chiun said flatly.

"Is not!" Remo flared.

"It is deadly. Do you covet my Masterhood so much that you would stoop to mere poison?"

"I did not—"

A single hand rose.

"It is one thing for you to covet my throne," intoned Chiun. "It is another to employ poison to achieve it. The House has not used poison since before the Great Wang. A simple blow while I sleep would have been sufficient—not that you would have landed such a blow or survived the attempt, but it would have been acceptable."

Remo shook his head. "You're being ridiculous."

"Am I? You would not be the first who attempted to supplant me as Master. You would do well to remember what befell him."

Chiun was referring to his nephew, Nuihc. His brother's son had been Chiun's first pupil. He had turned against his village and used his deadly skills for evil. Chiun had personally eliminated Nuihc in order to save Remo's life, and had mentioned the matter rarely over the past decade. The fact that he brought it up now only angered Remo more.

"Look," Remo protested, growing hot, "I'm trying to honor you here! Why are you giving me all this BS?"

"Because you are giving me poison duck. I will not eat it, and I suggest you do not."

"But you *gotta* eat the duck!"

Chiun drew back, his clear eyes hardening. His long-nailed fingers found his wrists and disappeared within the tunnel of his sleeves. He cocked his head to one side.

"I must?"

"It's supposed to be your *kohi*! Remember? This way you can turn one hundred!"

Chiun became angry. "I am only eighty!" he snapped. "I will always be eighty. I will never age, thanks to your white thick-headedness, and I will never die."

"You won't?" Remo asked, taken aback.

"I cannot afford to," Chiun squeaked. "For I am the last of my line, and my only successor is a pale piece of a pig's ear who covets the treasure of my ancestors."

Remo put his hands on his hips. "You know that isn't true. And I'm sick of apologizing for not realizing you weren't dead that one time. Pulling this 'poisoned duck' scam is a low move. I went to a lot of trouble preparing this bird!"

"Then you eat it," Chiun sniffed.

"I will," said Remo, reaching out to rip loose a shriveled brown wing. He brought it to his mouth.

The Master of Sinanju watched with silent interest. Remo's strong white teeth took hold of a string of meat and pulled it loose.

He had barely tasted the greasy meat when, faster than Remo's Sinanju-trained reflexes could avoid it, a nut-colored hand swept out. Remo thought for an awful moment that his front teeth had been pulled.

One moment he was tasting meat and clutching a duck wing. Then both were gone. Remo tasted the duck on his tongue and swallowed involuntarily.

As soon as the greasy morsel hit his stomach, he knew the duck was poisoned. His dark eyes widened with shock. One hand over his mouth, he made a dive for the bathroom.

After he had emptied the contents of his stomach—mostly stomach acid—into the toilet bowl, and his vision had begun to clear, he heard Chiun's voice, calm but interested.

"You did not know the duck was poisoned."

"Of course I didn't!" Remo snapped, wiping his mouth with the back of his thick wrist.

"Unless this was clever subterfuge to lull my newfound suspicions," Chiun continued thoughtfully, stroking his wispy beard.

"Then why'd you pull the duck from between my teeth?"

Silence. The pause lengthened. Remo got off his knees, which were rubbery from the after-affects of the shock to his highly attuned nervous system—and Chiun answered.

"Because I did not wish to be burdened with the disposal of your worthless round-eyed carcass."

And the Master of Sinanju swept from the room. Soon, the sounds of broadcast-quality British voices once again filled the apartment.

Remo moved swiftly into the living room and did something that had gotten untold hotel bellhops, apartment house superintendents, telephone repairmen, and other rude persons maimed or killed more effectively than if they'd stumbled across an organized crime summit in progress.

He switched off one of Chiun's soaps and stepped before the dark screen, blocking it.

Chiun's facial hair trembled. His eyes narrowed until they resembled the seams on old walnut shells.

"I bought the duck from the Japanese supermarket at the foot of the hill," Remo said in a dead-level voice.

Chiun looked up, his expression stiff, like that of a death mask.

"Consorting with Japanese," he said in a monotone. He shook his aged head. "It is no wonder you have gone astray."

"I can prove it!" Remo said heatedly. "I have the receipt, and the plastic wrapping off the duck. You know how long it takes to wash the aftertaste of plastic wrapping off fresh duck?"

"About as long as it takes to wash virulent poison and other evidence of foul play," Chiun said pointedly.

"Thank you, Jessica Fletcher," Remo said acidly. "Would you like to see the wrapper?"

"No. It has obviously been tampered with. It is a pink salmon."

Remo blinked. "Say again?"

"One of those mystery things," sniffed Chiun.

Remo, taken aback, gave this some thought. "You mean a red herring?" he asked at last.

"It is possible," Chiun said vaguely. "For although I speak excellent English, my American is not as fluent. No doubt it is the fault of certain officious persons who continually tamper with the tongue."

"I'm more interested in knowing who tampered with that damned duck."

"Ah. So now you cast blame on the poor innocent duck."

"No, I don't. But since you and I almost ended up like dead ducks as well, don't you think we should look into this?"

"Why?"

"Because the Japanese supermarket is the only

place for miles around here that carries decent rice."

The Master of Sinanju absorbed this observation. His be-wrinkled visage alternately twitched and smoothed, as the inchoate expressions vied to dominate it.

Firm resolve won. Chiun came to his feet and said, "Lead me to this place."

The Hinomaru Japanese Supermarket claimed to stock no foods or goods that were not imported from the islands of Japan. Its signs were exclusively in Japanese. Any person who spoke only English would have been lost in its well-stocked rows. Even the prices were in yen, although the dollar was welcome.

Non-Japanese were not barred from the Hinomaru Supermarket—that would have been illegal—but neither were they made to feel welcome.

So when Remo and Chiun entered the establishment and demanded to speak to the manager, they were pointedly ignored.

This rudeness lasted as long as it took for the Master of Sinanju to insert the head of a stock clerk into the gaping mouth of a deep-sea bass that was stacked in an ice-lined cedar counter in the seafood section.

When the stock clerk's muffled cries attracted the manager's attention, Remo grabbed him by his white shirt front.

"Speak English?" he asked.

"Yes. Naturarry."

"Great. I bought a duck here today." He held up the wrapper. "Where did this come from?"

"We do not serr these," the manager said, a little too quickly for Remo's liking.

"My ass," said Remo.

"I knew it," said Chiun. "You are in galoots together."

"That's 'cahoots,' " corrected Remo.

"Thank you for admitting your guilt."

"If you'll just use your nose, you'll smell the heady aroma of ruddy duck wafting through the deep-sea bass," Remo said pointedly.

Whatever retort the Master of Sinanju had been about to make was never offered. Instead he began to sniff furiously, then flew into a back room, where two stock boys were busy re-crating shrink-wrapped duckling corpses.

Chiun scattered them with a flurry of upraised arms, and fell upon the crates. He sliced a package open with a long fingernail and extracted a headless duck carcass. He sniffed it all around and said, "Poisoned." He dropped the duck from his tapered fingers.

Turning on the flustered manager, who along with Remo had followed him into the room, Chiun demanded, "From whence comes this carrion?"

"Japan," said the manager instantly. He nodded his head like one of those glass birds that constantly bob for water.

"You lie!" screamed Chiun, with such vehemence that Remo momentarily dropped the limp, bloodied wrapper he had been carrying. He snatched it up with a backhand gesture, one eye on the Master of Sinanju as he hectored the suddenly trembling Japanese.

The exchange that followed was too rapid for Remo to follow, even if he had been fluent in conversational Japanese. But the facial expressions told most of it. Chiun was accusing the manager of lying through his teeth. The accused protested, relented, and then shamefacedly admitted his guilt.

He slunk off, then promptly returned with a bill of lading. Chiun snatched it up, glanced at it, and blew out of the supermarket like an elemental wind, leaving Remo staring at the manager, and the downcast manager contemplating his own shoes.

Remo handed him the duck wrapper and said, "Nice chatting with you," before he left.

When Remo caught up with Chiun he asked, "Where are you going?"

"To the kingdom of the Chicken King."

"Yeah? Why?"

"To search for poisoned ducks, of course."

"Why on earth are we off to see the Chicken King over a duck?"

"That is not the proper question."

"Then what is?"

"The proper question is, 'Why is the Chicken King poisoning ducks?'"

"Could be worse," Remo suggested.

Chiun stopped and examined his student under the sickly yellow corona of the late afternoon sun.

"How?"

"They could be poisoning fish, too. Then we'd be eating rice and nothing but." Remo grinned disarmingly.

Chiun frowned. "Only a round-eyed white would entertain such a dastardly thought," he sniffed.

"Don't look at me. *I* didn't poison the freaking duck."

"That," said Chiun darkly, "remains to be seen."

"Oh," said Remo, who had thought he was off the hook, but now knew otherwise.

5

"Fast, powerful, and extremely virulent," pronounced Dr. Saul Silverberg, leaning over the operating table. He was dressed in the starched white uniform of a surgeon. He had on white orthopedic running shoes with white rubber soles, thick white athletic socks, baggy white, pleated slacks, a stiff white cotton shirt, and the classic white lab coat.

Over his mouth and nose was a white mask, attached by a white band around his white ears. Even his hair was white. He was with the Department of Poultry and Avian Sciences, Human Nutrition Division, School of Environmental Medicine, Latvia Nuclei Research Laboratory, New York Medical Center, which made him the foremost expert in food-borne disease outbreaks in the world. He involved himself only in the most important cases, had a reputation to match, and didn't come cheap.

Only the best in the world was good enough for this patient.

"Forceps," he snapped to the short brunette nurse. She slapped it into his hand. He worked briskly, carefully. "Probe." She gave him that, too. "Light," he said. "I need more light here."

The nurse repositioned the intense penlight on
the flexible metal stand closer to the patient's
mouth. Silverberg peered inside.

The operating room shone with new beige tile
and pink caulking. All the equipment was gleaming silver. It was all brand-new, perfectly maintained, and the best money could buy.

Silverberg looked up, his expression serious,
and pinioned the patient's guardian with his
milky gray eyes. "I'm ... concerned," he said
solemnly, choosing his words carefully. Then he
began spitting out terse questions.

"Where did she last eat?"

"Out ... outside," said the patient's guardian.

"Were the foods prepared hours before
serving?"

"Uh ... yes."

"Was there adequate refrigeration?"

"Well, no, not really."

"Was the food reheated?"

"No."

"What were the symptoms?"

"What?"

"Nausea? Vomiting? Cramps? Diarrhea?
Fever? Other?"

"Well, you saw her, doctor. . . ."

"Yes," said Silverberg grimly. "I see her." His
inquisition resumed. "Did you check the
utensils?"

"Yes."

"Water supply?"

"Yes."

"Sewage disposal facilities?"

"Yes."

"Garbage storage?"

"Yes."

"Vermin control?"

"Yes."

"Lighting? Ventilation?"

"Yes, yes, yes!" the guardian exclaimed. "We checked absolutely everywhere and everything. There just doesn't seem to be a reason for this terrible, terrible disease!"

Silverberg looked up from the operating table at the man opposite him. The latter was sitting in a small glass room, speaking into a state-of-the-art microphone. Dr. Silverberg listened through a tiny speaker set high on the tile wall.

The man had a light bulb-shaped head, fringed with yellow hair, and decorated with narrow eyes, a light bulb nose, and thin lips. He didn't so much have a chin, as a neck that started a few inches below his mouth. His neck was as wattled as a turkey's.

Although skinny, the man wore an expensive, beautifully tailored brown suit, which nevertheless sagged on him like a burlap bag. His tie was thin and power-red, tied in a wartlike knot under his bobbing Adam's crab-apple.

"Yes," the doctor repeated, straightening. "Well, there's not much more I can do here." He pulled off one white rubber glove with an audible snap. "Besides, the anesthetic is wearing off. Nurse, post-prep the patient."

The brunette started undoing the straps. The patient blinked several times, kicked her legs once, and clucked. The nurse stepped back as the specially bred fryer chicken tried to stand up.

Dr. Silverberg motioned the animal's guardian forward, while taking off his mask. Henry Cackleberry Poulette strode into the Henry Cackleberry Poulette Operating Room in the Henry Cackleberry Poulette Wing of the Woodstock, New York, Veterinary Hospital.

The man millions knew as "the Chicken King" from his series of award-winning commercials faced Dr. Saul Silverberg over a gurney. "Is she all right?" he asked. "Is my baby all right? Will they all be all right?"

The doctor shook his head slowly and sadly. "Serotype enteritidis," he said gravely. "S.E., for short. It is a very serious disease."

"You don't have to tell me!" Poulette exploded, his wattle neck stretching even longer. "I'm the one who introduced the legislation all but wiping out S.E. in our lifetime!" He looked at the confused chicken on the operating table, just beginning to stagger away from the tiny restraining straps.

"But how is it possible?" Poulette muttered. "I installed an in-plant chlorination system. I added the slow-release chlorine dioxide rinse...." His tiny eyes began to tear, and his Adam's apple began bobbing in time to his half-swallowed sobbing.

The chicken swayed on one leg, executed a half-turn, and plopped onto her scruffy breast.

"My poor, poor baby!" moaned Henry Cackleberry Poulette. "May I take her now?"

The veterinarian nodded.

Tenderly, Henry—Hank, to the world—Poulette lifted the chicken in the prescribed manner, like a football. Weeping tearfully, he carried her from the diagnostic room as Dr. Silverberg and the nurse followed him with their eyes.

"He so loves his birds," whispered the nurse.

"You would too," said Dr. Silverberg, "if you looked like a Bantam rooster."

"It doesn't seem to bother him."

"That's because he doesn't see the resemblance," Dr. Silverberg said flatly.

"You're joking. He plays up the resemblance on all his commercials."

"Because the ad agency people tell him to. He fires anyone who calls attention to the resemblance," Dr. Silverberg fixed the nurse with a professional eye. "You're new here. Remember that."

"Yes, doctor," said the nurse, who had been hired fresh out of the New York State College of Agriculture in Ithaca, New York.

Henry Cackleberry Poulette carried the ailing fryer to his awaiting limousine and rode in silence back to Poulette Farms Poultry & Foods, Incorporated. He entered the building alone, still carrying the sickly bird. He skirted the Kill Room and the Eviscerating Room and strutted quietly past his battery of secretaries like a man in mourning.

He closed the soundproof door to his office. Only then did he gently lay the chicken down on his immaculate desk.

He paused to dry his eyes with a breast-pocket handkerchief monogrammed, in lieu of initials, with the profile of a Brahma hen.

When his eyes were dry they went to the figure of the ailing fryer, standing on his desk blotter. It was shifting its head about to peer out the broad office window at the nearby Catskill Mountains.

While it was enjoying this view of the verdant New York countryside, Henry Cackleberry Poulette stole up behind it and, laying one hand over its beak to choke off any outcry, grasped the frightened fowl's neck with the other.

"Betrayer!" he snarled, then broke the neck with practiced skill and no more sound than a Number 2 pencil snapping. Then he turned the chicken's head completely around to finish her off. "You bumble-footed, egg-bound minx!"

The chicken kicked and flopped strenuously. Henry Poulette set her on the yolk-colored rug and watched her race blindly into the furniture, her dead, unseeing neck hanging like a deflated balloon.

When its legs started to jerk and hesitate, he gave it a savage kick, finishing it off.

"That's for Woodstock High School!" he spat, crushing the skull with the heel of one shoe. "And the senior prom! You and your kind made my childhood a hell on earth! To think that I fed you the best marigold petals money can buy!"

6

The scene at Poulette Farms Poultry & Foods, Incorporated, was reminiscent of Woodstock's most famous brush with history.

Several dozen placard-carrying protestors blocked the chain-link gate to the main office buildings, stopping visitors and hurling invective at Poulette employees. The protestors wore tie-dyed shirts, torn jeans, and brightly colored bandannas around their filthy, uncombed hair. Some were barefoot, and still more wore shabby-looking boots that appeared to be new yet were coming apart at the seams. Around their necks a few of the older protestors wore huge, gaudy peace symbols, which looked as if they had been fashioned in their junior-year metal-working class.

Remo parked his car in the lot marked for visitors, and he and Chiun cautiously approached the tangle of human jetsam.

Cries of "Poulette Farms is cruel to chickens!" were being directed toward the complex itself. Another faction was screaming "Reject Meat!" They seemed to be screaming at the animal rights contingent.

When the crowd was within breathing distance, Chiun's face twisted into a mask of disgust.

"Remo, did not your government outlaw these dippies years ago?" the Master of Sinanju asked, flapping a kimono sleeve in front of his nose like a fan.

"No," Remo replied, not bothering to correct Chiun. "I think they decided to let them go the way of the brontosaurus on their own—but the asteroid is late."

They floated through the outer ring of protestors.

"You know what they do to chickens in there, man?" a man demanded of them. He was pot-bellied, fortyish, and carried a sign that read REAL MEN DON'T EAT CHICKEN in his grubby hands.

"If it involves bathing, you should go to the head of the line," Remo suggested.

"Carnage!" cried a female protestor.

"Bloodletting!" shouted another.

"Torture!" screamed a third.

"Too bad there isn't more of that out here," Remo said.

He and Chiun tried to thread the line of circling men and women, but they were halted at nearly every turn. They easily could have forced their way through to the gate, but that would have involved actually touching the protestors. Neither of them had the urge to get that close.

"Make way or pay," Remo said finally. He danced around a woman with breath so thick it actually made puffs in the warm spring air.

"Meat-eater!" she snapped at Remo accusingly. She wore a T-shirt emblazoned with the legend AN ALL-NATURAL PRODUCT OF THREE-G, INC. Remo noticed that several of the protestors wore similar shirts. "Marrow-sucker!"

"Get plucked," Remo said.

"Do not talk to them, Remo," the Master of Sinanju hissed. "They are so ignorant that they think we consume the lowly chicken." He avoided the outstretched hand of another woman whose sign read MEAT IS MURDER.

"But you do eat some meat," the first woman accused.

"Some," Remo admitted. "Duck and fish."

"You feast on the flesh of our aquatic brethren?" she asked, shocked.

"Hey, I eat fish," said one of the younger men picketers. His placard read POLITICAL AMNESTY FOR FOWL.

The woman whirled. "Murderer!" she shrieked. "Anti-Vegan!"

The young man stepped back, stunned. "I thought fish was okay." He seemed on the verge of tears.

"Not if you're a fish!" the woman snapped.

"Aw, lay off the kid," inserted an older protestor. A few others voiced their support for the young man's diet.

"I saw you eating ice cream last week," someone accused the boy's defender. "You lactovo!"

"Ice cream ain't meat, man," the older man countered.

"But it comes from cows," another insisted. "A true Vegan refuses to ingest any animal product."

"Look who's talking, leather-shoes."

"Plastic falls apart."

"So does a cow, once you've ripped its skin off."

"They didn't tell us at Three-G that we couldn't *wear* the stuff," someone pointed out.

"Maybe that just proves they don't know everything at Three-G!" Remo's accuser crowed triumphantly.

"What is this Three-D?" Chiun asked Remo.

Before Remo had a chance to shrug, a grimy finger was extended between them, indicating a large, glistening building on a promontory above, overlooking the Poulette complex on the valley floor. "Three-G," the man intoned with an almost religious reverence. "Heaven on earth to all true Vegans." He turned back to the others.

A mini-shouting match ensued within the group. Remo and Chiun took this as an opportunity to slip through the crowd, past the small security booth and onto the grounds of Poulette Farms.

Behind them, one of the protestors was tearfully removing his leather sandals. Sobbing, he cuddled the tattered shoes to his chest as if they were a stillborn baby and blubbered, "But I'm a good herbivore!"

At the rear of the crowd, Mary Melissa Mercy lowered her sign.

Somewhere behind the brilliantly reflective windows in the building up on the hill, the Leader stood sentinel over the proceedings on the valley floor. She raised her hand in a quiet sign of victory, even though she knew the gesture to be futile.

The first trap was about to be sprung. The Leader's vengeance would be absolute.

Mary handed her placard to another protestor and hurried up the road to Three-G.

Getting inside the Poulette Farms office complex proved to be as trying as penetrating the gate, Remo found. A bored guard sat inside a bagel-shaped desk in the main foyer. Behind him were huge poster-sized blow-ups of a man with features that were most definitely poultry-like, surrounded by a bevy of beautiful women. The women were invariably blond, and the man was always holding a denuded chicken. They were still photos taken from Poulette's famous television commercials.

"Remo MacLeavy," Remo said, flashing a plastic badge that identified him as a Department of Agriculture inspector.

"And he is . . . ?" the guard asked, indicating Chiun.

"With me," Remo said coolly.

"I would see the Chicken King," Chiun demanded.

"ID?" the guard asked in a tired voice.

"I am Chiun. That is all you need know."

"Yeah, right," said the guard. He motioned to Remo. "You can pass. He stays here."

"C'mon, pal," Remo said. "He gets testy when he's held up."

"Sorry," the guard replied. "Not without proper ID. We've had a lot of trouble with these protestors lately," he explained.

"Do I resemble one of those cretins?" Chiun sniffed.

The guard sized up the tiny Korean. "Actually, you do look kind of old for a hippie. But then, the ones that are left are getting along in years too." He squinted and looked Chiun in the face. "How old are you, pops—a hundred?"

Wrong thing to say. Remo knew it the moment the words vibrated along his eardrums. But there was nothing he could do about it.

Chiun's eyes became as wide as pie plates. His

mouth fixed in an angry line. Remo took a pre-
cautionary step backward.

When they exited the lobby a moment later
the guard was lying atop his desk, his arms
pinned like wings in the sleeves of his jacket,
his legs trussed up and knotted together with his
dull-blue uniform tie. He looked for all the world
like a Thanksgiving turkey. A bony one.

The girl knelt in the center of the wide desk,
her head bobbing up and down in time with the
seated man's joyful cries.

"That's right," Henry Cackleberry Poulette
panted breathlessly. "Oh, do it, baby. Uh-huh,
uh-huh. Don't hold back."

"I'm doing it, Mr. Poulette," the girl complained. Her tightly wrapped derriere was jutting up into the air. Just then some of her long
blond hair escaped from the tangled knot at the
back of her head and dropped in front of her
face. "Oh, great," she complained, pulling the
now moist hair out of the way.

"Don't stop now!" Poulette screeched.

The secretary sighed, tucked her fists up into
her armpits, and began flapping them once more.
"You know, some people might think this was
kind of weird," she whined. She began moving
her head up and down once again, grabbing up
mouthfuls of corn from a feeding tray positioned
in the center of the desk's blotter.

"You aren't paid to think," Poulette said. He
had just finished up the job at hand and was
straightening himself up.

"No, I'm paid to act like a hen," the girl muttered, inching her way carefully down to the
thickly carpeted floor.

"I'll let another breeder know when I'm ready

again," Poulette said, with a dismissive flick of his scrawny wrist. "You may join the rest of the brood."

The girl had adjusted the seams on her form-hugging skirt, and was in the process of pulling the office door open, when an elderly Oriental stormed through it with a haughty flourish. He was followed by a handsome, almost cruel-looking man of about thirty, with thick wrists and the most exciting eyes she had ever seen.

"Hi," said the secretary, pulling her blond hair free from its bow and allowing it to spill around her shoulders in her most practiced provocative manner. She smiled at the young man.

"You have corn stuck in your teeth," Remo said, pointing.

The woman clapped an embarrassed hand over her mouth and turned her back.

"Who are you birds?" Henry Poulette demanded.

"You," Chiun declared, advancing on Poulette. "Chicken King."

Henry Cackleberry Poulette's neck extended from his highly starched collar like a jack-in-the-box. His head jerked spasmodically to one side, and his triangular lips squeezed into a pucker.

"Who the hell are you?" he demanded. Without waiting for a reply, he shouted at his secretary. "Breeder! Get away from that capon! And get some of my security roosters up here!"

Shaken from her distraction, the secretary darted away from Remo and into the outer office.

"MacLeavy, USDA," Remo said by way of introduction. He indicated the Master of Sinanju. "My associate. He's into ducks."

"Anseriformologist, huh? I don't see many of your kind."

"Your ducks are poisoned, King of Chickens!" Chiun accused. "You will explain this!"

"Ducks? We don't have ducks here." Poulette sat back down. "Poulette Farms produces the finest chickens in the world, but no ducks. They're waterfowl. I'm a poultry man. Strictly poultry."

Remo held out the bill of lading Chiun had acquired at the Hinomaru Japanese Supermarket. It bore, in fine print, the name "Poulette Farms." "Says duck here," he said in a bored tone.

Poulette shrugged his bony shoulders. "Must be a forgery. Not surprising. My name on a package of wings is good for a thirty-cent markup over my competitors birds."

"Liar!" Chiun slammed a palm down on the desk top with such vehemence that the desk separated at every joint and dowel, falling into its component parts all around Henry Cackleberry Poulette.

Poulette scrambled to his feet, blubbering, "No lie! Truth! Truth! Poulette Farms is the single greatest distributor of plump and juicy chickens in the United States! If you promise to leave now, I'll give you one! Best on the lot! Hell, I'll even throw in one of my secretaries!"

In a flurry of movement visible only to Remo, Chiun was around the wrecked desk and hovering above Poulette, his hazel eyes ablaze.

"Do you deny a conspiracy between yourself and my avaricious son?"

Poulette seemed bewildered. "Son?" he asked, glancing to Remo for assistance.

"That'd be me," said Remo, touching his T-shirt front with a thumb.

"For the moment," Chiun said over his shoulder.

"Never met him before in my life!" Poulette said quickly. "We've got a couple of dozen USDA inspectors at the plant during normal shifts, but he isn't one of them."

Delicate long-nailed fingers floated before the Chicken King's mesmerized face. "I will wring the truth from your scrawny neck," warned the Master of Sinanju.

It took Chiun's hand one-thousandth of a second to grab the jumble of nerves on the side of Poulette's neck. It normally would have taken Henry Cackleberry Poulette one full second to respond, but his nervous system could not process the pain that quickly—though his spinal chord almost overloaded itself with the effort.

"Ducks! Flocks of them! In the secret wing!" he cried at last.

"Secret wing?" asked Remo.

"And the poison is hidden in this secret wing?" asked Chiun.

"I don't know! Could be! I'll take you there! Right now!"

Chiun released Poulette's neck with a final squeeze, leaving the Chicken King gasping in pain. "Lead us," he ordered.

Poulette rose shakily to his feet and followed the two men from his office. The tight-faced Master of Sinanju led the way.

"You people sure do take your ducks seriously," he said as he walked beside Remo. He twisted his distended Adam's apple back over his shirt collar into a more comfortable position.

"Good thing for you that you're not poisoning fish, too," said Remo, closing the door behind them.

7

"You're lucky to be alive, Dr. Smith."

"It is probably just a minor allergic reaction, Dr. Drew."

"Hardly. You've been poisoned. And I understand there have been cases like this all up and down the East Coast."

"I am confident it is nothing serious," said Harold Smith, frowning at his green-and-white surroundings. A Folcroft hospital room.

"People are dying, Dr. Smith. I find that serious."

Harold W. Smith dragged himself unsteadily to his feet. He found his clothes, and pulled on his white shirt with pitiable difficulty. The doctor looked at him with concern. Smith tried to give a reassuring smile, but lost it somewhere in the effort. Not only was the CURE director unfamiliar with the expression, but his head had begun to swim uncertainly. The antiseptic room spun before his myopic gray eyes, and he was forced to steady himself against the wall. This from the strain of stepping into his trousers.

"You should rest for a few days," the doctor cautioned.

"I feel fine," Smith said curtly.

"Perhaps. But according to your records you have an enlarged heart and history of pulmonary trouble."

"You know full well the trouble has nothing to do with my heart," Harold W. Smith said brittlely.

The trouble had begun earlier in the day, in fact.

He had ignored the styrofoam cup Mrs. Mikulka had placed on his desk while he attended to more urgent business. The woman was efficient, but she was a little too willing to accept a person's word. Smith had checked with the cafeteria personally in order to make certain Folcroft had not been billed for the missing yogurt.

He then went back to monitoring CURE's computer lines. He had begun picking up spotty wire service reports of apparently random food poisonings. There was no pattern emerging. People were succumbing in restaurants, in their homes, at picnics, and elsewhere. Smith, who looked for patterns in his raisin bran, became engrossed in finding one here.

It was a full two hours before he turned his attention to the styrofoam container on his desk.

A yellow film of grease had formed on the top where the soup had congealed. Smith broke through the surface with a metal spoon he kept in his desk drawer—disposable plastic was out of the question. Too expensive in the long run. Metal cost one lump sum, and was reusable forever.

The chicken soup below was cold. Smith spooned a bit of the broth from just below the surface to his thin lips and tasted it carefully. He licked the spoon clean, placed it neatly beside the cup, and turned back to his computer screen.

It was ten minutes before the irresistible urge to vomit overcame him. Smith grabbed the empty wastebasket from beside his desk and promptly filled it with the meager contents of his stomach.

When he thought the retching had finally abated, it began again until it seemed that nothing more could be released. Still, he could not stop.

Hastily secreting his computer terminal back inside the desk, Smith summoned Mrs. Mikulka by intercom. She found him slipping from his chair like a gray, melting snowman, and alerted the medical staff.

They immediately pumped Smith's stomach.

It was now three hours later. Harold Smith's gray head felt light, and his throat was scraped raw from the tube that had been inserted down it. His stomach felt as if a Tonka toy had been using it as a racetrack.

"If you had eaten more than a spoonful, Dr. Smith, you might not be here right now," Dr. Lance Drew said, concern on his grim features.

"I *am* glad I did not eat more," Smith said, without a hint of irony. He labored to tug on his gray jacket.

"A man your age shouldn't push himself so hard," Dr. Drew said solicitously. "Take a few days off. Relax."

"Thank you for your concern, doctor," Smith said thinly, closing the door—along with the doctor's protests—behind him. He then began the long trek back to the administrative wing of Folcroft.

He had to stop and lean against the wall a half-dozen times for support. When he arrived at his office, Mrs. Mikulka bustled out from behind her reception desk.

"Dr. Smith, you should be lying down!"

"No!" Smith snapped, firmly. He inhaled once, the pain in his throat making the effort difficult. His voice regained its usual calm tone. "I am all right. Really. Would you please call my wife and tell her that I will be working late tonight?"

It went against her better judgment, but Mrs. Mikulka knew better than to contradict her bloodless employer. "Of course, Dr. Smith," she said, reaching for the phone.

As he sank painfully behind his desk, Harold Smith immediately called up his computer screen. A new wave of news digests had come in during his absence. All had been flagged "Top Priority." It was an epidemic now. Thousands had died in nearly sixteen states.

And it all seemed somehow tied to . . . chicken?

A distant memory tweaked at the back of Smith's consciousness. He prodded it, but nothing came to mind. He was still woozy.

He would have to trace the poison back to its source. Better put Remo on standby, he thought, reaching for the blue contact phone.

He allowed the phone to ring a total of forty-three times before he took the receiver away from his ear. There was no answer at the Edgewater condominium tower. Remo and Chiun were gone. He had no way to reach them. He calmly replaced the receiver in its cradle.

Smith returned to the incoming news digests. The epidemic seemed to be confined to the eastern seaboard and a few midwestern states.

He ran several analysis programs. None sug-

gested an explanation, but all offered the same
high-probability conclusion.

"My God!" Harold Smith muttered. "This is
product tampering on a scale never before seen!"

And the two men most able to stop the menace
were nowhere to be found.

Smith glanced down. On his blotter, the container of cold chicken soup and the metal spoon
still sat. Allowing himself a rare "damn," Smith
picked up both objects and dropped them into
his wastebasket.

The loss of the spoon brought fret marks to his
tired ashen face.

8

"Look," Henry Cackleberry Poulette began reasonably, "if there's a problem with my birds—and I'm not saying there is—it didn't necessarily start here. I ship my babies out to restaurants, supermarkets—even to the Asian market."

"We got ours in a Japanese supermarket in New Jersey," Remo said.

Poulette snorted. "Those crazy Japs. I gotta ship my ducks to Tokyo just so they can claim they're Japanese exports. Their customers won't eat homegrown."

"Maybe the problem started in Tokyo," Remo said to Chiun.

"Had to!" Poulette assented instantly. "My birds are number one USDA approved!"

"It is certain that the ducks were poisoned," Chiun said stiffly, eyeing Remo suspiciously. "We are here to learn at what point."

Remo only rolled his eyes heavenward. They continued their purposeful walk along the corridors of Poulette Farms Poultry & Food, Incorporated toward the abattoir.

"So am I to understand you eat a lot of duck?" Poulette asked Remo.

"Between Chiun and me," Remo said sincerely, "we probably keep your duck wing flying."

"But you don't eat chicken?"

"No."

"May I ask why not?"

Remo hesitated. His brow bunched up, casting a puzzled shadow over his dark eyes. "Little Father, why can't we eat chicken?" Remo asked.

"Because chickens do not urinate," Chiun replied.

"A foul lie!" Poulette interjected.

Chiun stopped. Slowly he turned, his eyes going cold. "You would dispute me, Chicken King?" he demanded slowly.

Poulette cringed at the term. "Well, technically it is true," he explained. Vindicated, Chiun began marching along the corridor once more, Poulette hurrying to keep pace. "Chickens don't urinate, per se," he confided to Remo. "They have no bladders, so their urine enters their bowels and is released with their manure. But they're just as clean as any other bird."

"We can't eat chicken 'cause they piss out their butt?" Remo whispered to Chiun.

"Remo, do not be gross," Chiun sniffed.

"Did you know that chicken has supplanted beef as the meat of preference in the United States?" Poulette began to rattle off statistics with growing pride. "Americans now eat roughly seventy-eighty pounds of poultry per year. That's thirty-four percent of the American diet right there, my friends. They only eat seventy-three pounds of beef, and that percentage is shrinking every year."

"Doesn't it go in cycles?" Remo asked. "Chicken this year, pork next year? People will be back to beef by the end of the decade."

"Oh, no!" said Poulette, assuming an injured tone, like that of a priest whose faith has been called into question. "The era of beef is over. Cattle are filthy creatures. Stomping around in their own feces. And pigs? I think the name says it all, don't you? Rooters in their own filth."

"What do chickens do out in your barnyard—float?"

Poulette allowed himself a condescending smirk. "Barnyard? Really, Mr. MacLeavy, you must be new with the Department of Agriculture if you think Poulette Farms is a barnyard operation."

They had come to a door marked OBSERVATION DECK 1.

"Let me show you how a modern poultry farm operates," Poulette said, an odd gleam coming into his gimlet eyes.

The door opened onto another, longer corridor. One entire wall was made of Plexiglas, broken up only by large steel doors placed every twenty-five feet along its length.

Poulette's step became more lively. "As you can see, this walkway takes us through every phase of poultry-processing." He pointed to a large door below. "The conveyor belt brings the chickens into the plant from our fattening and feeding rooms." Remo and Chiun watched as the belt slid a steady stream of live chickens, hung upside down by their feet, into the Processing Wing.

"They are then moved through the electrically charged solution that you can see below, which"—Poulette suppressed a sigh—"stuns them senseless." He swallowed convulsively, and his turkey-wattle skin danced over his jittery Adam's apple. "It is remarkably humane."

"They say the same about the electric chair,"

Remo said dryly. "All the same, I'd just as soon go in my sleep."

Poulette's eyes narrowed. "Are you certain you're with the USDA?"

"Let's see the killing room," Remo said quickly.

"Very well," Poulette said. He had long since given up hope that his security roosters would come to his aid. "There is no individual who performs any of the more . . . ah . . . distressing duties. Nearly everything in the system is automated," he added, stepping to a bank of controls. His fingers took hold of a trak-ball mouse and joystick.

"From here they are carried into the Kill Room, where their naked, helpless throats are expertly slit by mechanized knives," he went on. Tears began to course down his cheeks. "Oh, the poor, poor creatures." At the same time some sort of craving came into his rapidly blinking eyes, and Poulette began to spin the trak-ball and stab blinking buttons.

A limp line of jiggling fryers began to march through a forest of glittering blades. The blades went *whisk-whisk* as they sliced open wattled throats. Spittle began to drip from the corner of Henry Cackleberry Poulette's mouth. His eyes shone.

Chiun drew his pupil to one side.

"Look at him, Remo," the Master of Sinanju whispered. "He feigns grief for his charges, while secretly reveling in their slaughter."

"Hey, Poulette!" Remo called.

Henry Poulette continued his frantic manipulations. Blood spurted. Snapping knives severed chicken heads.

Remo yanked the Chicken King away from

the control board, saying, "What happened to automated?"

Poulette turned sharply to Remo. "And let someone else have all the—" He caught himself, swallowed twice. "This is the backup," he said meekly, the blood-lust draining from his eyes. "Just in case." He paused, smiling sheepishly. "I see that my birds are treated more humanely than by any poultry man in history."

Indicating the blood-spattered Kill Room, Remo growled, "It shows."

"Better me than someone without my love for them," Henry Poulette said in an injured tone. He straightened his tie. "Please follow me."

When they reached the next area, Remo and Chiun were forced to breathe through their mouths. The glass and doors were thick, but still the stench from below poured up into the narrow walkway.

"As you can see, the bleed tunnel is below." Poulette's eyes had become glassy and distant once again. "The red, red blood drains from their gutted throats in a vat of scalding water, which loosens their festering quills. Those clawlike instruments there automatically pluck the plumage from the unfortunate birds. What is left is then singed off by the hell-bath."

Remo and Chiun watched as the naked bird carcasses paraded past in a gruesome line, being drained, plucked, and flame-denuded all at once.

"Yours is a depraved society," Chiun sniffed.

"This setup *is* pretty sick," Remo agreed.

"Sick? Every time a chicken dies, a part of me dies with it," Poulette said. "No matter what those misguided protestors say." He made a noise that started off as a giggle but became a cough. He balled his fist before his face and hacked several times. To Remo, it sounded for all the world as if Poulette were cackling.

When he had composed himself, the tour continued. Remo shot Chiun a confused glance, but the Master of Sinanju seemed to be regarding Henry Poulette more intently than ever. As if he could read the man's innermost thoughts through the back of his eggshell skull.

"Coming up is my pride and joy, Mr. Mac-Leavy," Poulette announced. The words were followed by another cackle, which Poulette then tried to pass off as a cough with some more throat-clearing noises. "The Eviscerating Room!" he said in triumph. "Here the dead birds are gutted and disemboweled by our machines before being graded by government inspectors."

"And the ducks?" Chiun demanded.

"They pass through here as well," Poulette explained, pressing his nose against the glass like a five-year-old at an aquarium. As he stared below at the images of slaughtered chickens spilling their internal organs from their bloody body cavities, his bald pate began to perspire and his breath came in short, orgasmic gasps.

"Where?" Chiun commanded.

Henry Poulette was drawing the tip of his pointed tongue delicately across his nub-like teeth. "Huh?" He pulled himself away with difficulty. "Oh, over there." He pointed to the far wall, where a much smaller conveyor belt carried freshly gutted carcasses into the inspection area. "The duck wing isn't very big, so every bird passes through this common area."

Chiun peered intently through the thick glass. Remo joined him at his side. "What are you looking for?" he asked.

"Your accomplice," Chiun replied.

Before Remo could reiterate his innocence in any scheme to do away with the Master of Sinanju, he was silenced by Chiun's gasp of triumph.

"There!" he pointed, his voice rising to a victorious pitch.

"Where?" Remo and Henry Poulette asked in unison. Both followed the direction of Chiun's delicately aimed finger.

The line of USDA inspectors was busily scanning and stamping what remained of the birds as they streamed past. At the very end, a burly inspector was glancing guiltily from side to side. On the work area before him he, like the other inspectors, had a cloth which could be used to wipe his hands. Except he was wiping the cloth *onto* his hands.

A subtle difference many would have failed to detect.

As the carcasses paraded past, he would draw his hand across the cloth and then stick his index finger into the yellow breasts of several of the birds. After each cycle, he would drag his hand across the cloth once more and begin anew.

"Behold, the fiend!" Chiun proclaimed loudly.

"Allow me," Remo said, moving forward.

They were next to one of the metal doors that rested in the Plexiglas wall, and the force Remo exerted against its handle nearly exploded it off of its hinges. Hooking his heels along the sides of the metal ladder that extended from the opening, he slid the thirty feet to the main floor and hit the ground running.

Oblivious, the fiendish inspector continued his work. Rag, duck, duck, duck, duck, duck, duck, rag. He looked like an automaton. He continued to glance from side to side, but there was something odd about his movements, as if he were an animatronic construct rather than a living human being.

When Remo grabbed the man's powerful shoulder and spun him around, there was nothing in the inspector's eyes to indicate that he was frightened in the least.

The man had a dark complexion, five-o'clock shadow two hours early, and coarse hair sprouting from his ears and nostrils. His nose looked like it had been broken at least a dozen times. His hands were thick and callused. Their backs and knuckles were covered with thick black fur. He kept his right hand clutched oddly in at his chest.

"Time to crow, pal," Remo said.

The inspector only smiled vacantly. The eyes continued to scan the room. Something about this bothered Remo. The look should have been that of a cornered animal—indeed, there was something not human in the man's face—but fear was not mirrored in the eyes. The eyes were . . .

"*Gweilo.*" The word sounded even stranger emanating from those rubbery lips.

"That anything like *paisan*?" Remo asked.

A hand flashed toward Remo's exposed neck, the guillotine-shaped nail of the index finger glimmering in the light.

It was traveling in a flawless arc, and Remo had not yet registered the move. According to all of Remo's experience, this thug who reeked of garlic and onions could not possibly be moving that quickly. Only one trained in Sinanju could.

The nail was a hair away from slicing into Remo's throat when another hand shot into view. Remo was propelled backward through the slimy procession of duck carcasses as the Master of Sinanju descended on the poisoner like a typhoon.

Chiun clutched the thug's wrist in his hand. The man continued to thrust with his sharpened fingernail, but Chiun's vise-like grip held it at bay. The nail made futile circles in the air.

"I release you from your walking death," Chiun whispered into the man's cauliflower ear, and drew his own sharp nail across the bogus inspector's throat.

A puff of Halloween-orange smoke shot from the man's nose, as if from an angry bull, and still more escaped in a dry-ice film from the bleeding neck wound. He opened his mouth as if to speak, but before he could his eyes rolled back in his head and he collapsed to the floor of the plant.

"Dammit, Chiun, what the hell'd you do that for?" Remo complained, as he got to his feet and brushed beads of water and blood from his shoulders.

"He was the poisoner," Chiun explained, quickly dispelling the saffron smoke with his kimono sleeves. A fleeting cloud passed across his stony countenance.

"I'll buy that, but we never found out who put him up to it," Remo pointed out.

Henry Poulette drew up, panting. He stopped, stared down at the body on the floor, and collapsed for support against the partition that separated them from the other inspectors. "Oh, my God," he moaned, "You killed Sal."

Remo stood the Chicken King upright. "Sal?" he demanded.

Poulette's head snapped up. "Uh, Sal Mondello. He was one of our best in-house inspectors.

Been with us for years." His face was ashen. He weaved on his feet like a roupy hen.

"He a relative?" Remo asked.

"I wish it was only that. Without Sal, Poulette Farms might as well be a chemical waste dump." His tiny eyes refocused, and he lost another shade of coloring. "And when the big man finds out, we're *all* going to be chicken feed."

"That's it," Remo said. "Interrogation time." He propelled Henry Poulette past the body on the floor and toward the access ladder.

Chiun followed slowly, a determined frown etched across his wizened features. His hazel eyes were reflective, as if not seeing the world around him, but one within. A world of horror.

A single sibilant word escaped his parchment lips.

"*Gyonshi!*" he hissed.

9

The secretary who had played Mother Hen for
Henry Cackleberry Poulette met the trio as they
entered the poultry producer's outer office. She
had picked the kernel of corn from her teeth,
which she now showed off proudly. The flock of
young blond secretaries looked up in unison from
behind their desks.

"We found the security team, Mr. Poulette!"
the girl said urgently. "They were hanging upside down by their feet in a utility closet!"

"Not now!" Poulette hissed.

Remo propelled the office door open with the
flat of his palm and tossed the Chicken King
inside.

"Start crowing," he ordered.

"You know, I really take offense at all of this,"
Poulette said. He indicated Chiun, who stood by
the door in uncharacteristic silence. "My God,
he just killed a man!"

"Which usually means I take the next turn,"
Remo pointed out.

Poulette's head shifted back, nearly forcing his
Adam's apple through the wrinkled skin of his
throat.

"Mr. MacLeavy," he said, "the USDA doesn't

ordinarily send its agents out into the field to murder and threaten murder." He seemed to have been emboldened by the continued silence of the old Oriental with the deadly hands. His pugnacious mood lasted only until Remo used the same technique Chiun had used earlier. Poulette's neck muscles felt as if they were being shredded by rabid dogs. His mouth dropped open, and his pointed tongue shot out and wiggled in the open air in front of his face. He howled in pain.

"The truth!" Remo said tightly.

"I hate chickens!" screamed Henry Cackleberry Poulette. "Always have! Always will! They ruined my childhood! I couldn't date! I had no friends! Everyone called me 'Hank the Cluck.' It was unfair!" he sobbed. "I don't even look like a chicken!"

Remo and Chiun exchanged glances.

"Then why get into this business?" Remo asked, releasing the pressure of his fingers.

"You know how my ads say 'a Poulette chicken in every pot'?" Henry Poulette said conspiratorially.

"Yeah?"

"If they're all eaten into extinction, no one will ever compare me to a chicken again! Never! Ever! Again!"

Remo looked into the fevered eyes of the Chicken King and said in a calm voice, "The truth I was looking for is a little different." Remo squeezed even harder this time. "Who was Sal working for?"

"Don Pietro!" Poulette shouted. "Don Pietro Scubisci!"

At the door, Chiun's head snapped around.

Remo, his attention trained on Poulette, failed to notice the reaction.

Remo blinked. "Scubisci? The Mafioso?"

"Don't know!" Poulette howled. "Don't know!"

"Do better, or join your dearly departed flock," Remo warned.

"I swear—I don't know if it was Scubisci! Mondello could've been working alone."

From the door Chiun remarked, "He speaks the truth."

Reluctantly, Remo released Poulette's neck.

Poulette caressed his injured muscles. His wattle jittered with the agitation. "Sal was a plant." He shook his head to clear his thoughts. His head pecked at the air, and he took a deep breath. "You see," he added, expelling the air, "years ago, when I was starting this place up, I was having trouble with the union help. They were causing me so many headaches that I threatened to fire the lot of them and hire all non-union. Then stuff started happening. Trucks overturning while delivering my birds. Mysterious fires on my loading docks. And there were picketers everywhere. I was going to go under. If Don Pietro hadn't stepped in, I wouldn't have made it."

"Nice of him," Remo said dryly.

"Hey, my problems were solved!" Henry Poulette said. "He arranged a sit-down with the union, and everything went back to normal. In return, I gave one of the Scubisci subsidiaries the hauling and carting contract on all Poulette Farms refuse."

"Nice way to do business," Remo commented.

"It is better than some others," Chiun muttered.

Remo was about to ask him what he meant by that when Poulette continued, "Don Pietro asked me to put Sal on the inspection line. I think Sal was family—you know, blood family—but kind of soft in the head, so I put him on the payroll."

"So Scubisci is poisoning America," Remo said.

"No." It was Chiun. He was shaking his bald head.

"What do you mean, 'no'?" Remo asked. "He probably has some scam worked out where he sells the antidote to local supermarkets. He's our man."

"I agree with him," Poulette said, indicating Chiun.

"Big surprise there," Remo said, sarcastically.

"No. Listen. Don Pietro has too big a stake in Poulette Farms," Poulette continued. "Besides, Sal has been spending quite a bit of time up the hill lately. If there's anyone who put him up to it, it's those vegetarian loonies."

"Who?" Remo asked.

"You must have seen them on the way in," Poulette said. "The nuts with the 'Reject Meat' signs? They're from Three-G."

"What is this 'Three-G'?" Chiun asked, suddenly interested.

"A pain in the crop," Poulette responded. "The guy who used to run it, Gideon, was kind of offbeat, but friendly. A good neighbor, member of the local chamber of commerce, that sort of thing. Since he left, I don't know what it's become. Some sort of commune, I think. They started picketing me last week."

"We will go there," Chiun said firmly.

Remo frowned. "Whoa! Could you check that enthusiasm for a minute, and tell me where the hell it came from?"

"They are closest to this den of horror," Chiun said, reasonably. "And they did not wish for us to eat duck. Therefore, we must investigate these vegetable-devourers."

"Yeah!" Poulette's head bounced wildly. "Motive and opportunity! He's right!" He waved a bony finger at Chiun.

"Since when did you two get so chummy?" Remo demanded. He turned to the Master of Sinanju. "And I say it's Don Pietro, and we should be halfway to Little Italy by now."

"No," said Chiun, firmly. "We will go to this G-spot."

"Mind telling a fellow duck-aficionado why?"

"It is the logical place to begin."

"Logic, my ass," Remo said. "You're up to something. What is it? If this is another excuse to bust my balls over leaving you in the desert, I'll say it again. Sorry. Sorry, sorry, sorry. I apologize most sincerely. Now can we go?"

The Master of Sinanju lifted his brittle eyes to the face of his pupil. They softened ever so slightly.

"If you honor the man you call your father," he said softly, "you will go."

Remo was taken aback by the old Korean's tone. All he had heard from Chiun so far was carping. Carping about stranding him below the California desert. Carping about Remo's secret desire to supplant him as Master. Carping about Remo's embarrassing performance while he was Master. Carping about the color of the damned sky, and somehow blaming it on Remo. Now something had changed.

Remo heaved a sigh. "If I go up there with you, will you promise to get off my back about this *kohi* thing?"

"I would not make a promise I could not keep," Chiun replied.

And understanding that his pupil had already relented, he swept through the door like a tired wind blowing.

10

He felt tired. Tired, weak and old. Oh, so old.

They had denied him the Final Death. The one, great sweeping of the meat-eaters into Eternal Oblivion. The mass sacrifice had been intended to feed those who had passed before him in the Life from Death until the Great End when all that was would be no more. Only in the throes of the Final Death would he be allowed to join the others of his ancient Creed.

The Final Death was the sustenance that would nourish the undead in the womb of eternity.

He was the last of the *gyonshi*. The blood-drinkers of old China. It was his destiny.

But the Sinanju master had stopped him. He and his cursed *gweilo*. They had halted the Final Death.

He allowed himself an evil smile. His yellowed teeth were exposed to the light, like the mouth of a rotting jack-o'-lantern decorated with Indian corn.

Not halted, he reminded himself. Merely postponed.

The child had come to him before. Was it a minute? An hour? The Leader did not know. In the ceaseless dark in which he dwelt, time no longer mattered.

"It has begun, Leader," the girl chirped happily.

The Leader cleared the phlegm from his aged throat.

"It began before you were born," he instructed the girl he called 'Missy.' "It had its beginnings before my birth, before the birth of this strange land we find ourselves in. It began in the mist. In the distant past of two great Houses."

The Leader smiled wickedly. "Here, it ends."

The girl left him to his meditations. His one great desire returned to him then. The thing that drove him in his age, in his infirmity. A calling greater than the Final Death.

The extinction of Sinanju.

It dwelled in his thoughts like a half-remembered lover. Tantalizing. Alluring. Obtainable.

He allowed the delicious sensations to fill his mind with visions that could only be imagined.

Her presence was in the room with him again. Young, vibrant. Everything he was not. He knew it was she before she could speak.

"Missy," the Leader said, nodding permission for her to speak.

"They come."

Her voice was tight, concerned. Still a child.

The Leader nodded. An infinitesimally small move of his purplish, skull-like head. The head swayed in its continual side-to-side movement. "They have stepped into the Shanghai Web, as expected," he rasped.

"But they are coming here, not to Little Italy."

"It is of no moment. There is no strand of silk in the Shanghai Web that will not lead to the inevitable. Do you recall the edict of old?"

"Yes. 'Separate and conquer.' "

The Leader nodded again. "Do as instructed." His paper-thin lids slid unconcernedly over his sightless white eyes.

"Leader," Mary Melissa Mercy nodded. She backed respectfully from the room in her sensible white shoes.

11

The Three-G, Incorporated, headquarters was an ultramodern building with all of the accoutrements that would be expected in the main facility of the leading producer of health foods in America. It boasted solar-heating roof panels and a satellite dish, and, if the clouds of flies swarming overhead was any indication, it eschewed the use of environmentally harmful pesticides to protect its landscaping.

The Three-G staff was a throwback to another era.

They were the same types Remo and Chiun had encountered down at Poulette Farms. The only notable distinction was that the same seldom-washed individuals were now wearing white lab coats. Over the breast pocket of each coat was an emblem of three interlocking uppercase "G" 's, in lime-green stitching.

Remo and Chiun had entered through the side door of the hilltop packaging plant, with the Master of Sinanju leading the way.

"We will surprise the dastardly poisoners," he had promised.

"If we do," Remo growled, "I promise you ruddy duck every Sunday for the next year."

"You are either foolhardy or very addled."

"How about confident we're quacking up the wrong tree?"

"Then why do you follow, round-eyes?"

"My round eyes want to get this silly wild-goose chase over with as soon as possible, okay?" said Remo, checking his reflection in a nearby window. His eyes *did* look kind of squinty.

On the packaging floor, Chiun accosted the first employee they came across. This was a man of about forty, with a tangled mass of hair and a dull look on his face. He had a tag on his chest identifying him as "Stan." The name fit him about as well as his flannel shirt, which had burst three buttons in the vicinity of his expanding gut. The fourth was straining to the breaking point.

"I would speak with someone in authority," Chiun said.

"Hey, I'm shift supervisor," Stan replied. "At your service."

"Where are your poisons?" Chiun demanded loudly.

The potbellied man snorted, swatting at a pesky fly. "You've come to the wrong place, man. Three-G is all healthy and all natural."

"A transparent subterfuge," Chiun spat.

Remo looked around, and saw only wilted flower children stacking bundles of Fru-Nutty Bars into cardboard boxes for shipment to discriminating palates everywhere. The very air smelled of chrysanthemum sugar, which Remo had read was healthier than cane sugar even though it was the color of coal tar.

"Chiun, come on," he said. "It's some kind of candy factory, for crying out loud."

"Not candy, Mr. . . . ."

The voice was silky and lilting, and came from behind Remo.

As Remo turned, he half expected to see a halo. The woman was that much of a vision. She crowded her loose-fitting blouse, and looked as if she'd been poured into her modest, calf-length skirt. Her hair was a reddish-blond nimbus, like follicle fire. A light dusting of freckles danced lightly across her nose and cheeks, just under the incongruous mirror shades. They were green, and made her resemble a pretty insect.

Her lips parted, in a smile that showed off a row of dazzlingly white teeth. They matched her shoes.

"Call me Remo," Remo supplied.

The vision took a step forward. "You can go back to work, Stan," she said quickly. "I will attend to our guests."

Chiun stepped between his pupil and the bewitching redhead. "You are in charge?" he asked.

"I am executive vice-president of Three-G, Incorporated," she answered. "Mary Melissa Mercy is my name."

"Show me your poisons," Chiun demanded. He crossed his arms in punctuation.

"If your body craves poisons, Three-G is not where you will find them I'm afraid, Mr. . . ." She paused once more, but the Master of Sinanju made a deliberate point of not answering. Covering, she said, "We have nothing here that is not wholesome and natural."

"A likely story," Chiun said. "I will investigate myself."

"Feel free," Mary Melissa waved. "We're open to public inspection here. We've nothing at all to hide."

"I will be the judge of that," Chiun said, storming off.

Mary Melissa watched him go, her head tipped pensively to one side. "An interesting man," she remarked. "He reminds me of someone I know."

"Then I feel sorry for you," Remo growled. "He's a freaking time-waster."

One eyebrow shot up above the top edge of her mirror shades. "You do not wish to be at Three-G?" she asked.

"Lady, it wouldn't be my first choice," Remo said.

"Oh?" Mary Melissa raised a second eyebrow.

Remo took in Mary Melissa Mercy's perfect figure. "Maybe second choice," he admitted.

She laughed. Remo liked the way her chest moved with her humor. He was searching his mind for an appropriate one-liner, when she resumed speaking.

She took a mock-serious tone, saying, "Really? I wonder what could be more important than the two of us getting to know each other better?"

"Getting through the day without having him drop a guilt trip on my head the size of Mount Everest."

"I'm afraid I don't understand."

"That makes two of us."

Mary Melissa Mercy hooked her arm in Remo's. There was something exciting about her touch. It was more than mere warmth. It was almost electric. But Remo did have one question.

"What's with the gloves?"

Things had gone terribly wrong. More wrong, in fact, in the past year than at any time in the Master of Sinanju's long life.

It wasn't only that he had missed his *kohi*—

although that calamity was something that Remo deserved to hear about, and would as long as Chiun had anything to say about it.

It was after that, when the tables had been turned and Chiun had thought he'd lost Remo to the toils of the demon goddess Kali, during what the whites in their ignorance celebrated as "the Gulf War." That had been a wrench to his spirit that the Master of Sinanju had had a hard time dispelling from his thoughts. It was a subject he and his pupil had mutually chosen to avoid. Remo, because it represented a blank period in his life he would rather not have revealed, and the Master of Sinanju because, without Remo, he understood that the Sinanju line would end with Chiun.

It was not any of these things singly, but all combined. It was as if every force in nature—physical, natural, man-made, supernatural—had combined to send the ancient house of assassins spinning into oblivion.

And now this . . .

He had almost lost Remo again. The slashing fingernail would have inflicted a more-than-mortal injury. Remo had not even seen it coming, and he still did not realize how close he had come to a walking death.

The Master of Sinanju slid along the corridors of the ultramodern Three-G building in silence, his sandaled feet making not so much as a whisper on the highly waxed floors, his elongated shadow a stab of black behind him in the scald of light burning down through the huge glass walls.

It would have been too familiar, what had nearly befallen Remo. Painfully familiar.

For all his lecturing on Sinanju's past, Chiun had spent little time dwelling on his own.

As he walked, he allowed his thoughts to wander back through the years. Before Remo, before America. To the brief time youth had allowed him. The hours, days, months, and finally decades peeled away in flickering shades, at last replacing the muzzy image of ordinary recollection with a mental picture so sharp and clear it could have been recreated before his inward-looking eyes.

He was in Sinanju. The sky was the hue of blue steel. Streaks of white clouds painted the distant horizon. The wind blew in off the sea, the salt spray collecting in beads on his coarse black hair.

The eyes he peered through were his own, but they were a young man's eyes.

Above him stood another figure. Taller than the man the boy named Chiun would grow to be. His hazel eyes burned with the inner fire that was the sun source.

Chiun's father—himself a master of the deadly art that fed the poor fishing village on the West Korean Bay—was called Chiun the Elder.

His father seemed taller on this day. At this point in Chiun's recollection, the Master-to-be was kneeling. The clear eyes of his father were cold. For Chiun the Younger had neglected his training in order to play with the children of one of the fishermen near the unforgiving waters of the Bay. It was not the first time it had happened. Chiun had been an obstinate young man.

Chiun the Elder scolded the younger Chiun in severe tones—but there was a touch of humor mingled in his father's admonishing tone. They both knew it would happen again. For Chiun the Younger was still just a boy, and boys never understand the responsibilities of manhood until they grow into men themselves.

"As punishment," his father had told him, "you will repeat the thirty-seven basic breathing techniques."

They were in the third hour of the exercise when a commotion broke out at the edge of the village.

It began with a single shout, but soon others had joined the cry.

Chiun the Elder started for the village so quickly, young Chiun did not register his sudden evaporation until the Master was a full thirty feet away. With the grace of a gazelle and a speed five times that, Chiun the Younger followed.

They were nearing the outer houses at the edge of the shore road. An elder of the village, whose responsibility it was to safeguard Sinanju while the Master was away, was running toward them. There was much weeping and shouting behind him.

"Master of Sinanju, protect us!" a woman's voice cried.

"Where is the danger, that I may crush it to dust?" Chiun the Elder had called back, his voice charged with fury.

They were met by a confusion of shouted pleas.

The village elder accosted them at the outskirts of the ramshackle fishing village. There was a frenzied look in his eyes that frightened young Chiun. He circled the Master of Sinanju and his pupil, while baring his teeth and grunting strange inarticulations.

The villagers were coming out of their houses now, some holding the limp bodies of dead rela-

tives. Several more bodies lay unmoving along
the main street.

"He has killed many, Master," the blacksmith
accused.

"He will kill more! I am frightened!" a woman
wept, drawing her child close to her.

A wailing chorus went up. "Protect us, O Master! We beg you!"

"Kill him!" several implored.

The Master lowered his head. "People of Sinanju, I cannot," he said gravely. "For it is written that no Master shall raise his hand against
one of the village."

"But he will kill us all!" lamented an old
woman.

"You would condemn us all to death for one
man?" the basket weaver demanded.

And it was at that moment that the village
elder had lunged at young Chiun. His father's
hand sliced through the air like a falcon descending on a pheasant. A perfect line was
drawn through the man's throat, and he dropped
heavily to the thick dust.

The villagers gasped. They gathered first with
hesitation, then with increasing boldness around
the fallen body.

Chiun the Elder dropped to his knees beside
the stricken villager and gently cradled the
man's head.

The wretch looked up into the face of the Master of Sinanju, a ghastly cast of evil on his calm
features.

"The one you called master is not the true
master, people of Sinanju!" he cried. "The Leader
is master of all! The *gyonshi* die in life! The
Final Death nears! Reject meat! Prepare for the
hour of reckoning!"

At that, an exhalation of orange smoke escaped his throat with his dying gasp, to fade in the chilling air.

Woodenly, Chiun the Elder lowered the man to the ground and wept. The people of the village formed a curious ring.

Chiun the Younger could only stand and watch, helpless.

From the back of the gathering crowd the murmurs began. They rolled toward the inner circle, where the keen ears of the Master of Sinanju could pick them up.

"If he would kill him, he would kill us," the old woman whispered.

"He has shamed our traditions," the blacksmith agreed.

"He is a disgrace to Sinanju," the basket weaver added in a hushed voice.

The Master of Sinanju slowly rose to face the villagers. As one they drew away from him, pulling their shivering loved ones closer to them.

"People of Sinanju, hear me!" he intoned. "I have ended the suffering of the one that has brought death to our village, and though he required death, he did not deserve it. I will not excuse my actions, for there is no excuse. I will leave the village this day and attempt to make peace with my ancestors in the mountains, where I may die in atonement. Do not allow the shame of the father to pass to the son, for Chiun the Younger is now Master of Sinanju."

He took himself from the village that very evening, an outcast whose name would be erased from all official records kept by the village.

The last young Chiun saw of his father was a black-clad figure disappearing through a cleft in the hills to the north of Sinanju, his broad shoulders hanging in shame.

The new Master of Sinanju had awakened that morning a happy boy and ended the day a grieving man, and so learned one of the most sorrowful lessons of his life.

Although this was a day Chiun had relived many times, he thought he had locked it away for the last time more than a decade ago. Self-indulgence was not seemly in a Master of Sinanju.

But the image was there again. He held it for a moment in his mind's eye, feeling the cold wind of night on his skin, hearing the reveling of the villagers behind him as they celebrated their new Master and protector, feeling the onerous weight of five thousand years of tradition bearing down on his too-young shoulders.

He was at that time but forty years of age—a stripling, by Sinanju reckoning. His training had not gone far enough along, he knew, for him to fulfill his duties properly. He despaired.

And then out of the hills had come the venerable Master H'si T'ang, he who had trained Chiun the Elder, saying, "I am your Master now. And you, my pupil."

Chiun did not question the man, whom he had been told was dead. He only knew that his ancestors had been wise. The unbroken line that was Sinanju would remain unbroken. That was a moment of such emotion that it had dried the tears behind his eyes before they could form.

Long, long, long ago, thought Chiun.

The image faded into gauzy shapelessness and vanished.

He was back. Back in America. Back to be tested once again.

He would do for Remo what his own father had done for him. As he had done for Remo in times gone by. Protect him at all costs.

And the key to avoiding death was distance.

Chiun continued to stalk the halls of Three-G, Incorporated, a grim specter in search of poisons he knew he would never find.

12

Mary Melissa Mercy displayed her white gloves in response to Remo's question.

"Poison ivy," she said, smiling. "I caught a frightful dose during weeding duty." She noticed Remo looking around, his attitude bored and impatient.

"Are you a true Vegan, by chance?" she asked suddenly.

"Got me," Remo admitted. "I don't even know what a false Vegan is."

"False Vegans come in many disguises," Mary Melissa Mercy said primly. "The lactovo-vegetarian thinks dairy products are proper. But the lacto-vegetarian refuses eggs, but will consume milk products. Then there is the debased vegetarian, who allows so-called white meats to desecrate his holy stomach, but not red."

"No, I am not a vegetarian," Remo cut in. "Not by your definition of the word, anyway."

"How strange," she said, her brow knitting. "I haven't eaten meat in years, and I have developed the ability to smell a non-vegetarian. You don't have that odor about you."

"I'll bet that comes in handy around the ol' salad bar," said Remo wryly, who thought he detected the scent of blood on Mary Melissa Mercy's breath.

Mary Melisa Mercy smiled sweetly. "Shop talk," she admitted with a shrug. "I'm sorry."

"I met some of your people down the road," Remo said. "They seem very . . . dedicated."

Her smile broadened. "You mean 'fixated,' " she said. "That's understandable. To an outsider, we would seem a little strange." A skeptical look crossed Remo's face, and she laughed out loud. "All right, we seem like a pack of loons. But it's just the way we live. We've chosen the strict Vegan lifestyle in this community, and it suits us. It also doesn't hurt the image of our products. We live healthy, so you eat healthy. Instruction by way of example."

"This place is a commune?" Remo asked, surprised.

Mary Melissa winced. "Such an old-fashioned term. We do have sleeping facilities on the premises for those who wish to stay here, but most of our staff have families just like everyone else. They punch out and go home at five."

They were strolling along one of the many glass-lined hallways of the Three-G, Inc., complex. The place was a labyrinth of spotlessly clean windows. It looked modern enough to have a jump on the twenty-first century.

Remo sensed a living creature cringing in a corner. He turned, and stooped to pick it up.

"Yours?" he asked, stroking the back of an emaciated tiger-striped cat.

He held the creature out to her, but suddenly it began to spit. Fangs bared, it began to claw the air in front of Mary Melissa Mercy. She retreated, her hands going to her mirror sunglasses.

"I withdraw the question," Remo said.

"Sometimes I have that effect on animals," Mary said by way of explanation. Remo raised an eyebrow. "Actually, it belongs to one of the workers," she added quickly. "She's feeding it a strict no-meat diet."

"That explains the mange," Remo said, turning the animal loose. It scurried down the hallway, nearly tripping an approaching figure just rounding the corner.

Remo saw the new arrival's legs were smooth and flawless, escaping upward into an agonizingly short skirt. Her body was rounded and curved to beautiful perfection, her neck slender and long.

Her face, on the other hand, looked like she had spent the past twenty years pounding it on a flat rock.

"Ms. McGlone," Mary Melissa said, acknowledging the other woman, who thrust out a thick slab of computer printouts.

"Here are the storyboards the ad people came up with for us." The woman's voice was a bray, and her teeth jutted from her mouth at bizarre angles, Remo noticed.

"We're gearing up production on our new Bran-licious Chunk Bar," Mary Melissa explained to Remo. A thought suddenly occurred to her. "Oh, how rude of me. Elvira McGlone, Remo . . ."

"MacLeavy," Remo said.

"Elvira is in charge of marketing."

As they exchanged indifferent nods, Remo noticed McGlone's ten pointed fingernails. They had been painted a deep red, like broad hypodermic needles charged with blood.

She didn't give Remo a second glance. "I have everything set up for you in my office."

"Fine," said Mary Melissa, curtly. "We'll discuss it when I have a free minute."

"But I'm ready for you *now*. The ad people are anxious to get this campaign started."

"Later," said Mary Melissa Mercy. There was just a hint of steel in her voice.

Remo was surprised that a battle-ax like Elvira McGlone could be cowed so easily. But she lowered her head like a scolded child and stopped her arguing in mid-whine. She flung a halfhearted "pleased to meet you" at Remo before skulking down the hall.

After she had gone, Mary Melissa Mercy turned to Remo. "Elvira wants to make an enormous splash in the media. It's something Three-G has never done before," she whispered. "I think she expects the Bran-licious Chunk Bar to push us from the health stores into the mainstream. I can't really blame her. It is the creation of Mr. Gideon himself."

"He the owner?" Remo asked.

"*Was* the owner," Mary Melissa said, her voice sad. "He passed away recently."

"Too bad," Remo said. He had begun peering past her through the inner windows, where flies buzzed amid a profusion of greenery. Remo caught a flash of silver and blue. Chiun. Looking for poison in the garden. This could take all day.

"Three-G has been taken over by a simply delightful old gentleman with wonderful Old World ideas," Mary Melissa was saying. "I'd love for you to meet him."

"Some other time," Remo said. He was debating whether or not to tap on the glass. They had to get out of here and back on the trail.

"Please?"

"Sorry."

"But he's just like your friend."

"All the more reason to avoid him."

"Here," said Mary Melissa helpfully, "if you're looking for your friend, I can call downstairs and have him paged for you. My office is just around the corner."

Remo turned away from the window and shrugged. "Lead the way."

Mary Melissa Mercy's office was large and richly furnished. One entire wall was a window that opened to the lush garden beyond.

Mary Melissa crossed to her desk, leaned her rear against its gleaming top, and stabbed out a three-digit number on her phone. After issuing a brief command, she replaced the receiver.

"They'll let us know when they find him," Mary Melissa assured Remo. "In the meantime, it appears we have a little time to kill. . . ." She uncrossed her legs. In the briefest flash, Remo could see that she wore nothing under her skirt. "What do you think we should do?"

It was clearly an invitation.

Remo knew what he should be doing. He knew he should be collaring Chiun and getting out of this dead end. But as usual Chiun had some weird ideas of his own, and besides, there was something about Mary Melissa Mercy that Remo was finding strangely fascinating.

He wondered what color her eyes were.

The Master of Sinanju wandered aimlessly. Eventually, he would rejoin Remo and report that somehow the trail to the poisoners led to some other distant point. Tokyo, possibly. Remo would certainly believe that the Japanese were poisoning American ducks without further explanation. It would fit Remo's perception of the Japanese, as fostered by the Master of Sinanju's sage instruction.

Perhaps he could even entice him to Sinanju, eventually.

There, they would bide their time and draw strength until they were in a better position to strike back at the *gyonshi* menace. For now, it was too soon.

The Master of Sinanju's meanderings through the Three-G complex brought him to the very heart of the building. He had been drawn to this place by a scent.

It was most curious. At first he had thought his senses were playing tricks on him, but then he realized how ludicrous a thought that was. The rotten odor was pouring down the brightly lit hallways, drawing him to this place. Along with the numerous flies.

It was a garden as rich in beauty as any of ancient times.

It nestled in the center of the building, surrounded on three sides by walls of glass. Some of the trees were too large to have been planted here since the building's construction. The builders must have taken care to stack their sheets of glass around the existing plant life.

The flowers, plants, and herbs were glorious and gigantic. The colors were lush and lovely. The smell was nearly overwhelming.

The Master of Sinanju walked past rows of giant sunflowers, hanging orchids, clinging vines, and leaves so thick and full they reminded him of a tropical rain forest.

He peered up to the top of the Three-G building, and at the afternoon sky above it. Chiun stroked his wisp of a beard appreciatively. The structure, while ugly in the way that most Western architecture was ugly, did at least serve some function. The cunning design of the reflective walls made this place a most effective atrium.

Even in his state of discomfiture, Chiun was pleasantly surprised to find something of such rare beauty in such a barbaric land.

His pace livened, as he followed a gravelly path through a copse of gnarled birch trees to a cluster of blooming lilacs.

The massive shell of a dead oak tree slouched at the end of the path. It was black, but speckled with a million crawling red ants. Great sheets of bark had peeled away and littered the ground in decaying heaps. Its thick, barren branches clawed longingly at the sunlight.

Near the tree, Chiun bent at the waist to take in the beautiful aroma of the flowering shrubs. He pulled it deep into the pit of his stomach and released. He was about to inhale a second time when he noticed it.

There was a scent under that of the lilacs.

Chiun's nose wrinkled as he smelled it.

He stepped up from the path to the raised mound from which the lilacs grew, then passed through them, coming upon the tree trunk from the north side.

He saw the soft mound of overturned earth first. Not quite as large around as a manhole cover. It was positioned between two claws of gigantic black root. It had been there nearly a month, by Chiun's calculations.

A wide crevice spread twenty feet up the rotted trunk of the tree. The Master of Sinanju knew what he would find even before he looked up. When he did lift his eyes, a ghastly vision stared back at him.

Several feet up the trunk, nestled in the moist and crumbling fissure, the skeleton of Gregory Green Gideon peered down at him. The bones were bleached white, and the lipless mouth smiled all thirty-two teeth at him in a clean, shining skull.

The *gyonshi* burial method. This was the ceremonial manner in which they disposed of their victims.

The *gyonshi* were here. All around him.

With a coldness settling deep in the pit of his stomach, the Master of Sinanju realized he had delivered not only himself, but Remo, into their clutches.

Mary Melissa Mercy had removed her right-hand glove. She was drawing the nail of her index finger along Remo Williams' back. Not the sharpened edge, but the outside of the cuticle. She had done this several times, so that he would be used to the caress of the nail. So that he would not anticipate her attack.

Then quickly and carefully, there would be a single jab. As the Leader had commanded. He would be vulnerable to it by then. For she had been cautioned that the *gweilo* of the Sinanju master had many tricks in his repertoire.

It would be easy. Separate and conquer. First, the *gweilo*. Then the hated Master of Sinanju.

She was just about to do the deed when the ceiling-to-floor window collapsed in a pile of glittering shards.

It splintered from top to bottom with a massive cracking sound, and the pieces fell in an impossibly delicate sheet, like a waterfall, settling in perfect slopes on either side of the frame.

Through the barely scattered debris whirled the Master of Sinanju.

Recoiling, Mary Melissa Mercy pushed her fiery mane off her forehead and buried her fingernails out of sight in its follicle fire.

"Remo, we will leave," Chiun said imperiously.

"I'm kind of in the middle of something here, Chiun," Remo said pointedly.

Chiun dug his fingers into a cluster of nerves at the base of Remo's spine, and Remo suddenly had about as much interest in Mary Melissa Mercy as in reading the financial page of *The Wall Street Journal*.

Remo's face became twisted in anger and confusion. "What's going on, Chiun?" he demanded. "Besides sandbagging my social life?"

"You are welcome," said Chiun, but his cold eyes were trained on Mary Melissa Mercy, who sat open-legged and red-lipped atop her desk, her eyes unreadable behind iridescent green sunglasses. Without a word, she slipped from the room.

Remo wheeled on the Master of Sinanju.

"How the ding-dong hell did you find me in here, anyway?" he growled.

The Master of Sinanju shrugged frail shoulders. "It was not difficult. I merely followed the flies," Chiun stepped toward the door, threw it open, and said, "It is time to go."

"Since when?"

"The poisoners are not here," Chiun admitted.

"Oh, big surprise," said Remo. "When did that come in over the wire service?"

"We shall seek them elsewhere," said Chiun, flouncing through the open door. "Come."

"Not in this lifetime," Remo grumbled, following dutifully.

13

Favio "Buster Thumbs" Briassoli expected trouble. He had been expecting trouble ever since he'd returned to Little Italy and the service of Don Pietro Scubisci.

Favio hated to admit it, but the Scubisci family was not what it once was. There was blood in the water. And blood always brought out the sharks.

Of course, he would never dare to express his fears aloud. Not even to his longtime friend Gaetano "Johnny Chisels" Chisli.

"You think Don Pietro maybe left some of his marbles back at the hospital, Favio?" Gaetano had asked recently.

"I think you bedda shud your fuckin' mouth, Johnny, that's what I think," Favio Briassoli had responded. But the truth was, the Don Pietro he was working for wasn't the Don Pietro of the old days. Not even close.

When everything had seemed to be going to hell a few years back, and he and the rest of the Scubisci syndicate had gone to the mattresses against the Pubescio family of California, Favio Briassoli, like any well-trained Mafia soldier, had fought right alongside his fellow soldiers.

But when Don Pietro had lapsed into a coma after eating a tainted piece of fish, and Don Fiavorante Pubescio of California had taken over the Scubusci family, Favio Briassoli, like any small-time hood who broke kneecaps for a buck, understood it was time to lam out to someplace safe until things cooled off.

They didn't cool off until Don Fiavorante cooled off, as in "whacked out." And in his stead returned the man the best doctors at Mount Sinai had declared was trapped in a "persistent vegetative state."

Favio wasn't sure how it had happened. Don Pietro, once he had mustered his old crew, declined to go into details. But of one immutable truth, he was sure.

Don Pietro Scubisci was in charge again.

But like a deep wound that refused to heal, Don Pietro's mind was not what it once had been. His years of poisoned sleep had caused damage the eye could not see.

The business with a low-life from Boston named Tony "No Numbers" Tollini had been the first evidence of this Favio Briassoli had seen with his own eyes. Favio Briassoli still shuddered at the gruesome memory.

He had been the trigger man. He had splattered the brains of No Numbers Tollini all over the walls of Don Pietro's place of honor at the back of the Neighborhood Improvement Association building. Afterwards, the don had taken one of the greasy fried peppers from the stained paper bag he always carried with him, dipped the pepper in No Numbers' brains, and brought the soft, cheesy matter to his dry, brittle lips with relish.

"It was like he was trying a freaking cake at a

freaking tea party," Johnny Chisels said, once
they had exited into the fresh air of Mott Street.

"Shut the fuck up, Johnny," Favio Briassoli
had replied. He was busy expelling his lunch of
linguini and clam sauce into the gutter in front
of the Neighborhood Improvement Association
building.

There were other occasions that prompted
street talk—such as a recent interest in the ways
of the encroaching Chinese—but he was Don
Pietro, so these lapses in decorum were ignored.

As a reward for their loyalty, Don Pietro had
entrusted Favio and Gaetano with the job of
protecting his frail old life. And that's where
they had been for the past few weeks. Inside
the Neighborhood Improvement Association,
perched on hard straight-backed chairs on either
side of the front door, steeled for the trouble that
was now unavoidable because too many mouths
were whispering that Don Pietro was a weak old
man with no more of a mind than a squash.

This night it was warm enough that they could
have sat outside, but on the sidewalk they
would have been targets for drive-by shooters
and Feds with cameras. And besides, no one
came to the Neighborhood Improvement Association who didn't have business there, and no one
came to the plain wood-facade, steel-reinforced
door without quaking in terror at what the tiny
old shell of a man and his army of thugs could
do if he were displeased.

On this night, Johnny Chisels was on edge.
As he leaned back in the wooden chair, he kept
bouncing it back and forth off the wall behind
him.

He stopped bouncing long enough to ask, "You

think there's somethin' really wrong with him
this time?"

"Hey, I ain't seen nothing wrong, so shut
up," Favio had responded. "You wanna get us
killed?"

Johnny Chisels fingered the butt of the 9-mm
Glock pistol in his shoulder holster. He had
lifted the weapon off a Colombian hit the year
before, and he had treasured it ever since. Own-
ing a piece none of his friends could spell made
him feel worldly.

"And quit playin' with that foreign piece of
shit," Favio added. "It's gonna go off one of these
days, and take your fuckin' nose with it."

"Aw, lay off, Favio," Johnny Chisels complained.

Favio Briassoli had gone back to staring glumly
at the floor, and Gaetano Chisli had just gotten
up to stretch his cramped legs, when the front
door exploded inward in a million shards of
wood and metal, carrying Johnny Chisels with
it. The two became a red abstract painting on
the painted plaster wall behind.

"Come out, come out, wherever you are!" a
voice called from out on Mott Street.

Favio Briassoli was up in a heartbeat. His
chair clattered to the floor as he slammed his
back firmly against the wall to the left of the
door, his heavy Wildey Survivor .45 clutched in
his meaty palm. About a dozen other burly thugs
in ill-fitting suits came cramming into the small
foyer from back rooms, Uzis in hand and backs
dragging sweat marks across the thirty-year-old
wallpaper.

"What is it, Favio?" one asked, eyeing the remains of Johnny Chisels.

"Shut up!" Favio hissed.

They waited in silence, but nothing else happened.

Tentatively, Favio Briassoli pushed his arm out the door, weapon first. He'd come out firing, and maybe peg off a couple of rounds into whoever had done in Johnny Chisels. But before he had a chance to depress the trigger, his gun was plucked from his hand like a spring dandelion. It disappeared in a blur out the front door.

"What the fuck . . . ?" Favio demanded. His fingertips were tingling. He hadn't even seen who or what had taken the gun from him.

A moment later the large handgun rolled back into the foyer. Its long barrel had been tied into a neat overhand knot.

"This is wrong," a singsongy voice complained from outside. "We are not to harm any who dwell within this place without instructions from Smith."

"Since when did you become a pacifist?" the first voice complained.

Wondering if the Irish Westies were making a move—since very few Sicilians were named Smith—Favio motioned to two of his burliest men. They took the signal and rushed to the door brandishing their Uzis. They leapt out into the street, while the others listened anxiously. The weapons managed a few feeble burps, and then were strangled into silence. Somehow . . .

Weapon in hand, Favio eased to the gaping front door, keeping off to one side. He was about to order the next wave into the fray. He got as far as jerking his thumb toward the door, when something that felt exactly like a steel vise grips reached in and dragged him, thumb-first, out onto the pavement.

He rolled back into the hallway a moment

later, his spine knotted in the same manner as
his handgun.

Next a face appeared at the door. It was
youngish, about thirty or so. The man the face
belonged to waved once to the cowering pack
of mobsters, with an ordinary hand that was
attached to his forearm by an extraordinarily
thick wrist.

"Borrow a cup of ammo?" he asked cheerfully.

One of the gangsters opened fire, saying, "All
I got are fuckin' clips."

The first volley of bullets ripped into the walls
around the door, chewing up wood and spitting
fragments of plaster onto the well-worn carpet—
and incidentally, adding a few kinks to Favio
Briassoli's already knotty spine.

The man with wrists like baseball bats easily
dodged the leaden storm.

He was in the hallway now, advancing on the
startled group.

"Gee, all I wanted was a cup. That had to have
been more like twenty," he said.

He was too close now for their machine pistols.
They ran the risk of shooting one another in such
a confined space. A few pulled handguns. The
closest pair reached for him with their bare
hands.

Those with outstretched hands lost the hands.
The thick-wristed man simply collected them
like so many toadstools. The newly maimed
members of the Scubisci family dropped to the
floor, howling and cradling bloody stumps. There
were only four left standing. They stuck their
guns in the face of the intruder and squeezed
their triggers in unison.

Before the rounds left their chambers, their

bodies had hit the floor. Bullet strikes peppered the surrounding walls.

But nothing else. For the intended target had vanished from the convergence of bullets, to reappear off to one side.

When all was quiet, Chiun entered through what remained of the front door. He picked his way through the carnage, delicately raising the hem of his silvery kimono.

"Thanks a heap for all the help," Remo complained.

"I disposed of the one who gave orders," Chiun sniffed. With his toe, he indicated the pretzel-like form of the late Favio Briassoli.

"And left me with a dozen more."

"You are in need of practice," Chiun said, glancing around the foyer with narrow almond eyes.

Remo eyed the Master of Sinanju quizzically. "Since when?"

"Since your elbow was bent."

Remo blinked. He hadn't heard that particular gripe—one of Chiun's favorites back in the old days—for many years.

"What's so terrible about a bent elbow, anyway?" he asked.

"Pray that you never find out," Chiun said darkly.

"Let's go find the big cheese," Remo said, shrugging.

"I warn you, Remo," Chiun said coldly. "This is wrong. Emperor Smith will be most displeased."

"Then why'd you follow me?"

Chiun's dry, papery lips thinned. He said nothing. His gaze darted into the building interior warily.

The room was shrouded in semidarkness. Remo trained his senses on the far end, and a black-walnut alcove. Only one person was there. The breathing was coming shallow and labored, laced with a loose-larynxed rattle. Whoever was in there had to be extremely old, sick, or both.

Remo creaked the door open carefully.

"What family you from?" someone in the back of the darkened alcove called.

Remo glanced at Chiun, who shrugged. "Sinanju!" he called out.

"The Jews ain't got no business in Scubisci territory," the voice answered. It was a pained, phlegmy rasp.

A light snapped on in the black-walnut alcove at the rear of the room. The light was the banker's variety, with a green shade and old-fashioned pull chain, and it illuminated walls plastered with sepia saints. A withered hand drew back from the ivory cone of light, to settle in the lap of the figure seated behind the bullet-scarred walnut table. The other hand was rooting around inside a grease-spotted paper bag. The thick smell of fried peppers wafted up from the greasy sack.

"What do you want from me?" Don Pietro Scubisci croaked.

"Answers," Remo said, advancing toward the alcove.

Don Pietro waved his free hand in a casual gesture. The other hand remained firmly inside the pepper bag. "A man my age, he has more questions than answers, I am afraid," he said. His eyes remained downcast, and he seemed to be absorbed in the spectacle of a cockroach that was crawling across his scarred tabletop.

"That's too bad," Remo said. "Because questions I got, answers you're going to give. Starting with Sal Mondello and Poulette Farms."

Chiun had drawn near to Remo, protectively.

"Remo, do not harm him," Chiun hissed.

"What?" Remo asked, surprised.

"Your friend, he is a wise man," Don Pietro Scubisci said. He reached his other hand inside the bag and pulled out a wedge of fried pepper. As if it had plans of its own, the first hand continued to search the bottom of the bag. Don Pietro placed the pepper delicately on his slug-white tongue and chewed it with deliberate calm. "You should be like him—maybe you'll live longer."

"My friend doesn't speak for me," Remo said. He rounded the table.

"A shame," Don Pietro said, shaking his head. "He sounds to me a very reasonable man." He still had not looked up at Remo.

"You and your dead-end kids have been behind the duck poisonings upstate at Poulette Farms, right?" Remo demanded.

"Remo!" Chiun called, sternly. "Have a care."

"Ducks?" a smile spread across the old man's features.

Don Pietro Scubisci looked up. Under the soft spread of light cast by the banker's lamp, his watery yellow eyes seemed to be swimming in a sea of mucus. But there was something else about those eyes.

Remo had seen that look before. He was wondering just where, when the hand slashed out of the greasy bag. It slit the paper in a perfect vertical line and went for Remo's throat like a switchblade snapping out.

The highly polished nail caught a glimmer of light from the banker's lamp. It was guillotine-shaped. Remo saw that much. And it came back to him.

Remo William's body went on automatic. He dodged the don's hand in a quick sidestep, forcing it downward with a stabbing forefinger so that it struck the top of the table.

Brittle bones snapped under the force of the blow, but it made little difference to Don Pietro Scubisci. Remo's other hand shot out like a pile driver, crushing the old don's face to a pinkish pulp. All residual brain activity ceased, as if disconnected from its power source.

The old man collapsed to the floor, the side of his face mashing against his bag. It disgorged slimy peppers across the tabletop, like scurrying green mice.

Remo wheeled on Chiun, whose hands retreated into kimono sleeves.

"Now you know. . . ." Chiun intoned, his eyes bleak.

"Mondello too?" Remo guessed. "Am I right?"

Chiun averted his eyes.

"Dammit, Chiun, why didn't you tell me?"

"I was awaiting the appropriate time," Chiun responded.

"When would *that* have been?" Remo shouted. "When one of them had carved me up and used me to trim a tree?"

At that, the Master of Sinanju's stern face became angry. Wordlessly, he crossed to where the body of Don Pietro Scubisci lay on the floor and knelt beside it. With one of his own sharpened fingernails he opened a gash in the dead man's throat. Amid the feeble gurgle of blood, a tiny puff of orange rose from the orifice to be swallowed by the banker's lamp.

Remo watched the vanishing smoke in wonder. "What was that?" he asked.

"The only way known to release a spirit from its walking death. By liberating the bad air that makes them so." Chiun rose to his feet. "Learned at great cost," he added quietly.

Remo stared down in disbelief at the corpse on the floor. The Master of Sinanju turned to face his pupil.

"Is there anything you would like to say to me?" Chiun inquired.

"Yeah," Remo muttered, shaking his head. "I wish I'd bought fish."

"Idiot!" Chiun hissed, flouncing about and floating off. "Round-eyed idiot! Dense as all your kind!"

"Hey, it was just a freaking joke!" Remo said, trailing after.

The body of Don Pietro Scubisci stared dully after them. It gave a final gurgle, from its throat rather than its mouth, and its limbs began to loosen and stretch in death.

14

"Chiun, wait up!"

Remo caught sight of the Master of Sinanju a few buildings down from the Neighborhood Improvement Association. There were no sounds of approaching police cruisers, which should have been dispatched to investigate the gunfire. As for the neighbors; they seemed strangely disinterested. As if they had their own notions as to what constitutes neighborhood improvement.

There were signs all around that Little Italy would be only a hazy memory in a few short years. If Chinatown was allowed to grow unchecked, it would continue to devour the Italian section of Manhattan like a hungry beast, building by building.

Mott Street was a strange collection of commingling ethnic smells. The odor of steamed milk and tomato sauce vied with pungent soy sauce for supremacy.

"Little Father. Time out. Okay?"

The Master of Sinanju froze on the sidewalk in front of a small food store. Inside the large glass display window, heavy tubes of prosciutto spun lazy spirals beside cured pork strips. A Chinese shopkeeper was whisking the sidewalk with an old-fashioned straw broom. His eyes squinted in haughty disdain at the sight of the unfamiliar Korean, and he began to sweep the sidewalk with increased vigor.

"Why didn't you tell me who was behind this?" Remo demanded angrily, storming up behind Chiun. "We could have stopped this before it got this far."

"Are you blind?" Chiun shouted, wheeling. "The *gyonshi* are a threat to us now only because of your ineptitude."

"*Gyonshi?*"

"It is the name the blood-drinkers use for their own kind."

"Oh, so these Chinese vampires are all my fault, are they?" Remo demanded. "What, did I forget to close the tomb after me?"

"I would not put such perversity beyond the realm of the possible," Chiun said. "Especially from someone of such obviously deficient parentage. But it is clear to me that had your stroke been pure fifteen years ago, we would not be facing this menace today. You have always had a problem keeping your elbow straight."

"Ah-hah!" Remo shouted. "*Now* I know where the bent elbow came from!"

"Yes. It came from you."

"I tell you, my elbow was straight!" Remo demonstrated a rapid stroke in the air before him. "Zip, zip. In and out. I shaved enough of his brain to keep the Leader in a coma forever."

Chiun's eyes narrowed. "Demonstrate again," he commanded.

Remo thrust his hand out before him at the same imaginary target. He stepped back, his face pleased. "There!" he said triumphantly.

"And this is identical to the technique you used on the Leader?" Chiun prompted.

"A perfect recreation," Remo said, folding his arms across his chest. "I haven't changed that lunge in fifteen years."

"Thank the gods we did not rely on that particular stroke against all of Emperor Smith's enemies," Chiun said curtly, "or there would be a veritable army of dispatched enemies pounding down our door."

Remo dropped his arms to his sides. "What's that supposed to mean?"

"The forward thrust," Chiun commanded. "Execute it."

Dutifully, Remo shot his arm out, forefinger extended stiffly.

"Hold!" Chiun ordered. Remo froze in position. "Now, return." Remo's hand snapped back to his side. "You bend on the return," Chiun said, his voice sour and flat. He seemed more disappointed than angry.

Taken aback, Remo snapped, "My arm is straight on the initial line. That's the power thrust. The return is only mop-up. There's no need to finesse it." The Master of Sinanju narrowed his eyes in disapproval. "It's all right to bend your elbow on the return," Remo insisted. He paused. Chiun stared stonily. "Isn't it?" he asked, deflated.

"You were supposed to immobilize the Leader to prevent him from taking his own life, for it is written that only in death is a vampire truly alive. Your sloppiness only wounded him. The brain has healed itself."

"You can't fob all this off on me!" Remo said hotly.

"Was it I who used the faulty blow on the Leader, back in that dry city of ten-quart hats?"

Chiun said aridly. "Was it I who placed him in that hospital of greedy quacks, and entrusted his caretaking to the insane Emperor Smith? Yes, Remo, I am fobbing. But it is I, Chiun the Fobber, who should be blamed for the fact that Sinanju will end with us. And I mean this, Remo. I am most sincere. It is my fault, for it was I who entrusted such an important task to lazy white help." Chiun now began to pad remorsefully down the street. "I should have performed the duty myself, but how can the young learn if they are not given opportunity? You were too callow. I should have known this."

"I haven't come through this without a few scrapes as well!" Remo called after him. "That old hairbag in there just tried to harpoon me!" he complained.

Chiun paused. "Yes," he said thoughtfully. "Thank you for that as well. I will have to explain his death to Smith."

"What's to explain?" Remo demanded. "This guy was *capo di tutti frutti* of the whole frigging Manhattan Mafia, and I took him out."

"Have you forgotten? It was Smith who arranged his ascension to power. A cunning move, because it installed a weak, ineffectual bandit chief in place of the more dangerous man who came before."

"So? He can install another old hairbag. Big deal. They're a dime a dozen."

"That is the least of our concerns at the moment," Chiun said, heaving a sigh. "This all could have been avoided. Had I not been such a kind and forgiving teacher you would not have lapsed into your slothful, corner-cutting American ways." His parchment face hardened. "That is not to say it is still not all your fault, because it is."

Remo was shaking his head slowly.

There came a sharp clatter, as if something had fallen, followed by a low growl behind them.

The busy Chinese shopkeeper had dropped his broom to the sidewalk and was advancing on Remo and Chiun, his right hand slashing and jerking before his own fierce face. Remo saw his *gyonshi* fingernail making deadly circles in the air.

"What is this—Night of the Living Take-Out?" he exclaimed.

Chiun was sliding off to one side, his hands free, alert to attack. "The Leader is diabolical in his ways," he cautioned. "He has set traps for us wherever we venture."

"Yeah, and he must have spent the last decade breeding like a bunny."

Remo and Chiun moved in such a way as to contain the shopkeeper in the shrinking space between them. As he realized he was being trapped he reacted feverishly, slicing first at one, then wheeling and stabbing at the other. Remo and Chiun dodged the attacks easily, but neither moved to stop the man. They were Sinanju, and understood that the speed of the dead thing before them was equal to their own.

It was clear that Chiun wished for Remo to dispatch the man, but there was something in the *gyonshi*'s eyes. The same dead light had been in the eyes of the bogus chicken inspector Sal Mondello and Don Pietro Scubisci. The Chinese was not in control of his own actions.

"Why do you hesitate?" Chiun asked Remo. He faded back just as the shopkeeper's index finger whizzed past his face, barely missing the Master of Sinanju's tuft of beard.

"It isn't this guy's fault he's like this," Remo said. He avoided a thrust by skipping to one side. The shopkeeper spun back on the Master of Sinanju.

"Pah!" Chiun said, disdainfully. "You are in need of practice against these vermin. If you wish to be merciful, end its suffering."

"Like I have a choice," Remo muttered, moving toward the wild-eyed shopkeeper.

A frantic voice came from across the street. It was high, lilting, although distinctly male.

"Master of Sinanju, behind you!" it called.

Remo had sensed the approaching danger, as he was certain Chiun had. A stocky Chinese woman of about fifty was stomping out of the entrance to the shop, her *gyonshi* fingernail pointed at Chiun like a deadly mini-lance.

The shopkeeper's wife, Remo figured. He looked about, in search of the author of the warning. He caught a fleeting glimpse of a figure in black. Then, he turned his attention to his own adversary.

Reacting, Chiun grabbed the female *gyonshi* by her plump wrist and seemed to exert only an easy tug. The woman's feet left the ground and she orbited once around. As she passed him, Chiun's other hand flew out and her throat slashed itself open on the outstretched fingernail.

Centrifugal force deposited her against a light pole, where she slid slowly to the sidewalk, her arms and legs bent at crazy, impossible angles.

It would have seemed to any onlooker as if the pair had simply performed a rather flamboyant dance step, after which the woman had sat down to catch her breath.

The orange mist seeped from her open throat.

"You are free now," the Master of Sinanju told the broken corpse without malice.

Satisfied, Chiun turned away. His wrinkled face smoothed in shock.

For there was no sign of his pupil.

"Remo!" Chiun called plaintively. "My son!"

And far in the back of his mind, he remembered the words of his ancient enemy.

The words were, "Separate and conquer."

Remo used his thick wrists to block the driving nail of his foe. But the *gyonshi* was stubborn. With the first parry, he cracked a wrist bone against Remo's wrist. He tried again. Another bone broke.

The hand hung off the fractured wrist like a drooping sunflower. The man's flat face also drooped.

Defeated, the Chinese shopkeeper ducked inside his shop. Without hesitation, Remo went after him.

He found the man trying to claw his way through the thick, triple-locked security door in the back storeroom.

"Sorry, pal," Remo said, spinning the man around by the shoulder. He slashed at the exposed throat, but his fingernails—although capable of cutting glass—weren't long enough to pierce pliable flesh, and Remo was forced to use a box-cutting razor against the man's yellow throat. He felt like a ghoul—Masters of Sinanju were forbidden the use of weapons.

Remo waited until the body had vented its puff of orange smoke before he left.

When he emerged into the sunlight a moment later, a crowd had already begun to form around the shopkeeper's wife. Ignoring the commotion, he glanced up and down Mott Street.

It was deceptively quiet. People passed in and out of doorways. Horns honked. Children shouted.

A lone squad car had arrived to investigate the disturbance at the Neighborhood Improvement Association.

But there was no sign of Chiun.

Remo's heart gave a leap of fear.

From somewhere, he seemed catch a whisper on the wind. The whisper seemed to be in Chiun's squeaky tone of voice.

And the words the wind seemed to whisper were, "Separate and conquer."

15

The aged door creaked in a slow and deliberate complaint as it was opened, the rotted wood around the hinges threatening to tip the warped slab of wood back out into the musty hallway at any moment.

The single bare bulb clicked on, illuminating the cluttered living area.

Chiun stepped in.

He stood in a long, musty room covered in bookshelves, work tables, and display cases. Hung along the walls were yin-yang symbols, warped circular mirrors, tattered bamboo umbrellas, rusty swords made of beaten Chinese coins, and the eighteen legendary weapons of China— including esoteric swords, spears, sais and nunchuks.

"I must apologize, for I did not expect to bring the Master of Sinanju home with me," said the creature the Master of Sinanju had followed to this place. He wore a simple black tunic, black kapok pants, and black Chinese slippers.

The man was thin, with a square face, a round chin, flat nose, and beady, amber, almond-shaped eyes. His hair was the color and consistency of wheat, but the most remarkable thing about him was his eyebrow.

He possessed but one. It stretched across his brow and dropped on either side of his face almost to his shriveled cheeks, like a frame of bristly hair.

Chiun picked his careful way through to the center of the shabby living room carpet and stood in stony silence.

The door creaked shut behind him, blocking off the sounds of a strident argument in a neighboring apartment.

"You do not need to thank me for warning you of the *gyonshi* female," intoned the creature.

Chiun's countenance remained impassive. "And I will not," he replied flatly.

A heavy pause clung like fog to the room's damp air.

"You know of me, then?"

Chiun's head turned, ever so slightly. "You are the Taoist with one eyebrow," Chiun responded. "An embalmer of Chinese. You are familiar with the ways of the dead—living or otherwise."

The Taoist with one eyebrow kowtowed elaborately.

"I am called Won Sik Lung," he murmured. "Like you, I have ancestral obligations. Like you, I am a sworn enemy of the *gyonshi*, who were thought extinct."

Chiun returned the bow with a studied nod of his aged head. "You will tell me what I need to know that I may vanquish the vermin known as the Leader," he said coldly.

The single eyebrow crept upward in surprise.

"You must have seen him around here somewhere!" Remo was saying, his voice urgent.

"About this high? In a silver kimono? No? Damn!"

The Chinese girl skipped off, leaving Remo to prowl the byways of Chinatown. He had no idea where Chiun had gone off to. He had vanished.

It would be like Chiun to do something like this, just to teach Remo a lesson. With Chinese vampires popping out of every doorway, Chiun decides to pull a disappearing act.

"This had better be a stunt," Remo muttered to himself. "Please let it be a trick designed to teach me a lesson," he whispered.

With a shiver, Remo suddenly thought of the orange wisps of smoke that had slipped from the throats of the poor Chinese couple behind him. This was no lesson. Chiun was gone. And Remo was getting that cold feeling again. The one that reminded him that Chiun was now a hundred years old, and had not been quite the same since he had been brought back from the dead.

Remo crossed to the opposite side of Mott Street. Voices called out to him as he ran, but they were drowned out by the commotion coming from around the Neighborhood Improvement Association. The first cruiser to arrive must have seen the bodies in the foyer and called for backup. There were also two ambulances parked beyond the rim of squad cars.

Suddenly Remo remembered something. A voice. *Master of Sinanju, behind you!* it had shouted.

He had caught a glimpse of a man. A Chinese, dressed entirely in black, like a mortician out of some old Western. He was tall, but Remo had gotten no impression of his face. Not that it would have helped. Despite long years of association with the Master of Sinanju, Remo still thought all Orientals looked pretty much the same.

Great, he thought: Excuse me, have you seen an old Oriental gentleman in a kimono, about five feet tall, in the company of a slightly younger Oriental dressed entirely in black?

What did they look like? Like Orientals. What else?

He felt foolish thinking it. But it was his only lead.

The first person he asked was a middle-aged Italian woman, sitting in a lawn chair outside a corner store.

"Yeah, I seen 'em," she said casually, as if the pair were a couple of bankers out for a stroll during their lunch hour.

"You did?"

"You did say one was Korean, right?"

"How do you tell the difference?" Remo wanted to know.

The woman shrugged. "Same way I tell a Sicilian from a Neapolitan. Anyway, they went east on Canal. Say, whaddya doin'? Leggo my hand!"

Remo released her hand. "Just checking your fingernails," he said. He darted down the street.

"My ancestors know well of the *gyonshi*, O Master, for though Sinanju has faced them a handful of times in its glorious history, we have encountered them many, many times. For us it is an honor to sacrifice our lives to thwart this pestilence."

"Speak not to me of Chinese honor, Taoist," Chiun spat. "My ears bleed."

The gaunt embalmer's single eyebrow furrowed at its center, like a black caterpillar scrunching up on a leaf. He lowered his head in an informal bow. "I am confused, great Master. Did you not come to me for my knowledge of the *gyonshi*?"

"I came for a single answer, Chinaman," Chiun responded. "And for this I may forgive the impertinence of your last utterance. If it is the answer I seek. Otherwise ..." He let the threat hang between them.

The Taoist seemed genuinely frightened. Good, Chiun thought. I have gotten the deformed creature's attention.

The Taoist cleared his throat. "You would defeat the Leader?" he asked, his tone making it clear that the question was unnecessary. Chiun merely stood in silence.

Like a nervous animal, the Taoist began glancing around the room. He stepped over a few scattered books and newspapers with Chinese printing, to a single door in the corner of the living room. It was tucked away behind a tattered easy chair. The door had once been painted green but the paint had long since peeled away, revealing a ghostly veneer of its original varnish.

"Come—into my personal sanctum," he bid.

The Taoist pushed the door open. The room beyond was deeply shadowed. Lights from a hundred white ceremonial candles danced along its walls.

"I will tell you all I know, Master of Sinanju," he said, ushering Chiun inside.

"Then perhaps I will spare your life, Taoist with one eyebrow," Chiun responded as he passed inside.

In the flickering candlelight, unnoticed by Chiun, a sparkle of light danced on the quicksilver sheen of the Taoist's index fingernail.

*   *   *

On Canal Street, Remo found three others who had noticed the path taken by the pair of Orientals. All indicated the same general direction. As they pointed Remo inspected their fingernails for the telltale guillotine shape, but none of the other passersby bore the mark of a *gyonshi*.

Remo was accosting a roasted-peanut vendor when a police officer came into view amid the crowd of pedestrian traffic. For a moment the cop seemed startled, but then he drew his revolver and aimed it carefully at Remo. "Hold it right there," he ordered nervously.

"No time," Remo said absently. Chiun must be nearby. But there were a dozen possible doors. "Did you see them?" he asked the vendor urgently. "A Chinese and a Korean, together?"

"You better *make* time, pal," warned the cop, his voice growing threatening. "A guy fitting your description was seen up where the Scubiscis hang out, just after the mass murder."

"C'mon," Remo prompted the apron-clad man, "I don't have all day." He continued to ignore the cop, who stepped forward with increased belligerence.

The vendor swallowed, uncertain. He glanced from Remo to the cop, then back to Remo again. He gave a feeble shrug. "Sorry," he mumbled. "I don't know from Koreans. I'm still gettin' used to all these chinks."

The cop had his handcuffs out and was moving up on Remo. "You're coming with me."

"Sorry, pal," Remo said, turning. "You've become a distraction."

Remo's hands shot out, slapping the handcuffs away and plucking the weapon from the startled cop's outstretched hand. Simultaneously, Remo stabbed a pressure point at the side of the man's thick-muscled throat.

The young policeman's pistol clattered to the sidewalk as he himself slid to the pavement. Remo propped the unconscious man against the side of a parked car. He focused his attention back on the vendor.

"Oriental in kimono. Oriental in black. Which way?"

"Uh, there," the vendor said, pointing with a trembling hand. "They were heading for that building."

He pointed to a brick apartment building, with some kind of black-curtained storefront on the first floor. A sign over the glass read WON SIK LUNG—EMBALMING.

"Thanks!" Remo called after him. "And clean your fingernails!"

.

Upon entering the smaller room the Taoist had lit another of the many thick candles, his right hand hidden from view in the long sleeves of his midnight-black tunic.

"For you, Master of Sinanju," he said. His bow this time was more formal.

Chiun returned the bow with the slightest nod of his head.

The Taoist now stood at one end of a low wooden table that sat in the room's center. The flames from several dozen candles danced in the lazy air currents of the room, where a bowl of black blood had been positioned carefully between the candles. Several worn pillows were spread out on the floor around the taboret.

The Taoist beckoned Chiun to join him.

Reluctantly, the Master of Sinanju gathered

up his skirts and knelt before the taboret. Only then did the Taoist himself fall to his knees.

They faced one another across the taboret, smoking shadows worrying their grim features.

"You have heard in your travels, O wise Master of Sinanju, of the blight upon this land known as AIDS?"

Chiun merely nodded. The embalmer went on.

"There have been some who have accused the *gyonshi* of introducing this virus, but it is known to affect far too few in its current form. Perhaps, in years, it will swell into a pestilence, but the Leader no longer has years. The *gyonshi* Leader craves the Final Death, and would not settle for less."

"I know of their methods," Chiun responded stiffly.

"But it is not known to many that the vampirism which affects the Leader's minions is a virus much like this AIDS. It is transmitted from one *gyonshi* host to another, by means of their own blood seeping up from beneath their fingernails. Enough of the poison remains in their bloodstream that they may contaminate victims forever. It is in this manner that they recruit innocents to do their bidding. And there is only one sure method of purging the host to the *gyonshi* poison: liberating the bad air."

"The orange smoke," Chiun said, nodding. He was staring at a faraway point in his past.

The Taoist nodded as well. "Your thoughts are of . . . ?"

Chiun's head snapped up. "My thoughts are my own, Taoist," he said with contempt. His eyes were angry slits.

"I meant no disrespect. . . ." the Chinese said quickly.

"I would know how to stop the Leader," Chiun demanded. He had had enough of this insolent embalmer. "Speak, Chinaman, or I will wrench your viper's tongue from your head, and with it flog your miserable carcass."

The Taoist with one eyebrow gave a jittery jump. Chiun was secretly pleased. Perhaps this loquacious creature would finally cease his meandering and come to the point.

The fear on the Taoist's face melded with resolve. He leaned toward Chiun across the small table, careful to keep his right hand out of view.

"Come closer, Master of Sinanju," he beckoned. "That I might whisper to you the secret of eradicating the *gyonshi* scourge forever. . . ."

The building was a hundred-year-old crumbling brick edifice that stood seven stories high. Inside, Remo found himself in a narrow hall made up of concrete bricks. They were painted a gaudy black, and over this was a painting of a long, coiling scarlet-and-jade dragon that led up a listing staircase.

There was no fast way to search the building. Remo vaulted up the creaking, rotted stairs to the second-floor hallway and began opening doors, locked and unlocked.

Curious Chinese faces craned out into the hallway. Those who had had their doors splintered open recoiled in fear. None belonged to the mysterious Chinese in black.

"Sorry, wrong number," Remo said by way of apology. He left the puzzled tenants in the second-floor hall and took the flight of stairs to the third floor in three steps.

He began splintering locks again. His face reflected great worry. Chinese vampires were dangerous. And the Master of Sinanju, although wonderfully recovered from his ordeal, was still not yet the Chiun of old—if he ever would be so again.

And even a Chinese vampire could get lucky, Remo knew.

If Chiun's tales could be believed, they had decimated Sinanju in times long ago.

Chiun, Reigning Master of Sinanju, had many things on his mind. Not least of which was the ignominy of having come to a mere Chinaman for help. But as long as Remo never learned of this, it would be between Chiun and his ancestors.

He hoped to return to the street before Remo could locate him. It would do the boy good to worry. From worry, comes appreciation.

"It is obvious that the Leader intends for the Final Death to sweep America," the Taoist was saying.

Chiun nodded. "He attempted to poison American cattle years ago, when this land gorged itself on beef."

"And in this slightly more enlightened age, he has visited his foulness upon fowl," added the Taoist.

"You know of the poisoned ducks?" Chiun demanded, surprised.

"Not ducks. Chicken. Word has traveled to Chinatown. The dead are many. I expected something of this sort. So many years . . . nothing. And then an outbreak of *gyonshism* more than a decade ago in Houston. Many Chinese call upon the family of Won to ensure that their ancestors rest easy and motionless. Much good blood and bad air was released. Then, quiet again. Until now. *Gyonshi* are abroad in Chinatown, and elsewhere. And elsewhere, men die from eating the flesh of chickens."

Chiun frowned, understanding that the Final Death could be achieved only through huge numbers. Chicken might accomplish this—but not duck.

Yes, the Leader wanted the Final Death, longed for it as he never had before, but he now desired something even greater. The destruction of Sinanju.

The Leader knew the special dietary requirements of a Master of Sinanju. There could be no other reason to baste ducks with one of his filthy *gyonshi* poisons. Americans, thinking they were eating healthier, were consuming more chicken—not duck.

"The duck was meant to flush Sinanju out into the open," Chiun murmured aloud. "It was intended that Sinanju should go to the Chicken King. The first trap lay there. The second at Three-G. A third at the stronghold of the Roman, Scubisci."

"Sinanju is not so easily bested," the Taoist said in a servile tone.

The Master of Sinanju waved aside the flattery. Chiun would protect Remo, but now that his pupil knew of the *gyonshi* threat he could be left alone for a moment. While Chiun conferred with the legendary vampire-killer.

"Speak, embalmer. How may I strike at these vermin without bringing risk to my own house?"

The Taoist leaned closer. His single eyebrow rose higher on his pale amber forehead. The candles that were spread around the darkened room cast weird shadows on his long, funereal face.

Chiun leaned closer.

The Taoist's lips pursed, as he prepared to impart the secret of the Leader's fatal weakness to the Master of Sinanju.

The Master of Sinanju looked into the candlelight reflections flickering deep in the Taoist's amber eyes.

The eyes!

But the hand was already up. Over the table. Across the space between them, like a viper.

Chiun felt a brush against his throat. Very light. No pain.

Too late . . . The Master of Sinanju had recognized the eyes too late.

A cloud of black descended over the room as the Taoist leaned back, eyes burning with a wild light. Then the cloud descended over the Taoist as well, blocking him from view. The cloud was everywhere in the room, but it was not in the room. It was in Chiun's mind, and his mind was accepting the darkness like a long-awaited shroud—and that shroud was somehow comforting.

And then the blackness was everywhere, as the last light of consciousness flickered and died.

The Master of Sinanju slumped to the floor.

On the fifth floor a man and woman were having a knock-down, drag-out over something. From the smattering of Chinese Remo understood, he gathered that it had to do with the husband's interest in a very young female employee at his place of business. The woman cried and screamed alternately, the husband yelled and apologized. Glassware broke in punctuation.

The fight must have been going on for some time, because the fifth-floor neighbors were slow to respond to Remo's persistent knocking. When they did peer out, Remo didn't see the black-clad Chinese among them.

There was one door that failed to open. Remo cocked an ear and listened. There was someone inside. A man. Breathing oddly.

But he was alone.

Remo was about to spring up the next flight of stairs when he heard it. It was more shallow than usual, but the intake of air was unmistakable.

"Chiun!"

Remo cleaved the ancient door in two with a single downward stroke and burst into the apartment beyond.

A living room piled high with clutter greeted his anxious eyes. Remo wasted no time there. The breathing had come from farther back in the apartment.

Another door. This one he wrested apart on its hinges, as if it were moist paper. Door fragments spun through the air like shrapnel, embedding themselves in the walls on either side of the inner room.

Remo saw the body on the floor. Its back was to him, and it was curled in the fetal position, but Remo recognized the emerald dragon design woven on the back of the silver kimono.

"Chiun!" he breathed.

The thin figure from the street knelt above Chiun. The one who had warned them of the female *gyonshi*.

He looked up at Remo, his eyes those of the most vile demon from hell.

"The one you look to for guidance will help you no more, *gweilo*," he laughed. "The hour of the Final Death is come."

Bile rising in his throat, Remo fell upon the

Taoist. Hands flew in a furious blur. Arms pounded with pneumatic precision. In seconds, the Chinese had been reduced to a quivering cone of jelly encased in its own black shroud.

When the body fell still, Remo drew the Taoist's own *gyonshi* fingernail across what had been his neck. In the shimmer of the candlelight, a puff of orange smoke rose and vanished.

He dropped to his knees beside the Master of Sinanju, holding the fragile head delicately in his lap, and said, "Not again, Little Father! I swear I won't lose you again!"

Tears squeezed from the corners of his pained eyes, as he gathered up his frail burden and bore him out of the bric-a-brac-littered apartment and down to the street below.

No one attempted to stop him. They all saw the expression on his face.

16

It was a unforgivable breach of security, but
Remo had threatened to take Folcroft apart,
brick by brick, if Harold Smith did not comply
with his demand for an immediate medevac.

The Coast Guard emergency rescue helicopter
touched down on the widest, flattest roof in Chinatown, where Remo stood, holding the Master
of Sinanju in his arms.

Less than thirty minutes later it alighted on
the sloping lawn of Folcroft Sanitarium, near the
decrepit docks on the edge of Long Island Sound.

Smith realized that medevacing a patient from
lower Manhattan, at a time when the police were
trying to clean up a gangland massacre, would
be difficult to explain. He hoped he would not
find himself in that position as, stooping, he met
Remo under the sweeping helicopter blades.

"I have been trying to reach you all day,"
Smith said, by way of greeting.

Remo glared at him. "Congratulations," he
said flatly, pushing past the CURE director.

The medical technicians had already been instructed how to carry the old man on the
stretcher. They were not to drop, jostle, bounce,
shake, or drag the old man. They were to do

nothing that might cause the old Oriental any further injury. The young man named Remo had explained all this to them on the way from the city. When one of them told the young man not to tell them how to do their jobs, he informed them that they hadn't been listening properly and explained the entire procedure over again, this time dangling one of them out the open door of the rescue helicopter by his ankles to focus their attention.

When they climbed off the helicopter in Rye, the technicians carried the old Oriental as if he were a gossamer chrysalis, not a mere human being.

Smith followed a grim Remo Williams across the broad lawn. He was having difficulty keeping up with the young man. His belt hung loose, for his stomach still pained him.

"What happened?" Smith demanded.

"Poison," Remo shot back.

Smith paled visibly. "He did not eat chicken?"

"He did not," Remo snapped.

"Good."

"This is a thousand times worse."

"Remarkable," Dr. Lance Drew said, shaking his head in amazement.

"What is it, doctor?" Smith asked.

Dr. Drew started, as if surprised by the reminder that there was someone else in the room with him. He had forgotten, he had been so caught up in his work.

"It's simply incredible, Dr. Smith!" he said. "This gentleman is obviously terribly, terribly old, yet his reflexes are those of a man in—" He paused. "Actually, they're not like a man's at any age at all. His reflexes are astounding. Pulse, heart, respiration. He's a phenomenal example of human longevity." Dr. Drew peered down at Chiun's motionless form. "No doubt a strict vegetarian," he added.

Smith and Remo stood on the side of the bed opposite the doctor. Remo watched in tight silence, rotating his thick wrists absently, as Chiun's thin chest expanded and deflated with each breath.

"Yes, of course," Smith said, steering the doctor to the point. "But we are more concerned about his prognosis."

The doctor stood upright and heaved a sigh. "Coma," he said, simply. "The patient has been exposed to some form of toxin, I suspect. I can't be certain. See this?" He indicated a tiny pink mark on Chiun's throat. "That is the site of the infection. Has to be. When did this happen?"

"About an hour ago," Remo said, looking up. His deep-set eyes were filled with concern.

The doctor shook his head. "Impossible," he said. "That is scar tissue. The scab has already fallen off. The puncture must be at least a week old."

Smith cleared his throat. "That will be all for now, Doctor," he said hurriedly.

Dr. Drew took the hint and began to leave. "I don't know what this poison would have done to a person not blessed with his constitution," he said, indicating Chiun. "It's his nervous system that has been attacked." He shook his head slowly as he stared into Remo's pleading eyes. "There's nothing I can do for him. I'm sorry."

Smith closed the door after the doctor and approached Remo cautiously. "I, er, know what he means to you, Remo," he said, nodding at Chiun.

"Don't start, Smitty!" Remo snapped. "You

don't have a clue what he means to me! So don't even bother!"

Smith cleared his throat again. The action still gave him considerable discomfort. "There is also the matter of the poisoned chickens," he said.

"You mean ducks. And how'd you know about them?"

Smith frowned. "I have had no reports about ducks having been tampered with. Only chickens. The death toll now stands at nearly two thousand individuals. What kind of madman would attempt wholesale poisoning?"

As this sank in, Remo's face twisted in anger. "Damn! This is all your fault, Smith!"

"I fail to understand," Smith said vaguely.

"Houston? Fifteen years ago? That ring a bell?"

"Not quite . . ." Smith said.

"Houston General Hospital," Remo explained. "That's where I put the Leader fifteen years ago. Remember the Leader? Old? Wizened? Blind? Out to poison all meat-eaters, because he belonged to an ancient Chinese cult of blood-drinking Chinese vegetarian vampires?"

"My God," Harold Smith said hoarsely. "Of course, it is the same pattern. Only this time it's chicken instead of beef."

"You were supposed to underwrite his medical bills," Remo continued in a biting tone. "Well, you obviously let that tiny responsibility go to hell for a few measly bucks. That's the only explanation. You would have known he escaped, otherwise."

"If you will allow me to get a word in," Smith said frostily.

Remo went on, as if unhearing. "You did this, Smith. You did it to all those innocent people.

This"—he pointed a shaking-with-rage finger at the Master of Sinanju—"is your fault. All because you were too freaking cheap to pay to clean the Leader's bedpans."

Smith's usually unflappable personality began to flap. "The Leader?" he muttered, his tired gray eyes blinking furiously.

"He escaped the hospital, and he started his 'Final Death' crapola all over again," Remo said flatly.

"The Leader?" Smith repeated, sounding more shocked than surprised. "But Remo, that is impossible."

"Oh, really?" Remo asked, planting his hands on his hips. "And why is that?"

"Because," Harold Smith said in a prim, colorless voice, "the Leader is safely confined here at Folcroft."

17

Elvira McGlone felt like an outsider now.

Not that she hadn't felt like one since her first day at Gregory Green Gideon's Three-G, Incorporated. She simply didn't fit in. Never had. Elvira McGlone wore tailored business suits and severe skirts, while everyone else wallowed in tie-dyed jeans and bandannas. She ate pastrami sandwiches and drank tap water, while the others ate Three-G's bowel-busting health bars and drank bitter foreign bottled water because they believed every stream and reservoir in America was polluted.

Elvira McGlone had thought things might change when the new owners took over. She recalled the old adage "a new broom sweeps clean," and fervently hoped that this new broom would sweep the rest of these retrograde hippies right back to the Age of Aquarium—or whatever starry era had spawned them. But if anything, the Three-G staff had only become more cliquish, leaving Elvira McGlone even further out in the cold than she had been.

And the worst, the absolute worst, thing about the whole affair, was that she was the one who had let the pair of them in.

It had happened right after what was to be her final meeting with Gideon, at which she had argued for better merchandising of their products. She had left her market projections in her Volvo and had gone out to get them.

When she had opened the entrance door, they were standing there. Just standing there. A redhead in a crisp nurse's uniform, and what was surely the oldest man in the world this side of Methuselah. They must have been staring at the closed door and when Elvira McGlone opened it, they stared at her.

"Do you invite us in?"

It was the old man who had spoken. Elvira figured they must be strung-out health freaks looking to take one of the free tours that Gideon gave to the public. He was forever giving away free samples, too, eating away at the Three-G bottom line.

"Why the hell not?" Elvira had muttered. "We welcome the halt and the lame, why not the blind and creepy?"

Elvira McGlone held the door open for them as they entered the Three-G building. They sniffed the air like dogs.

"We couldn't have come in unless you asked us," the redheaded nurse chirped inanely.

The elderly man—he looked Chinese—only smiled at her. His eyes were white as pearls and his breath smelled like he'd just swallowed a recently expired skunk.

Shaking her head, Elvira let the door swing shut behind them and went out to her car to retrieve her papers. She thought that it would end with that.

It didn't.

Somehow, that very week, the creepy pair had

assumed ownership of Three-G. The stockholders, who consisted mainly of Gideon's fellow wallowers in granola, had installed them unanimously. Elvira McGlone was not told what had happened to Gideon. Her queries were met with blank-eyed evasions, even from the usually talkative veggie zealots, who until then had been a happy assemblage of Vegans and lacto-or lactovo-vegetarians.

Now they chanted "Reject meat!" and had become irredeemably macrobiotic.

It was all much too bizarre, even for Three-G.

Elvira McGlone clomped along the hallway nervously, her long, bloodred talons striking time on the back of her clipboard. It was funny how the place made her so uneasy now. She found herself missing Mr. Gideon. She felt bone-cold every time she thought of him.

She steadied herself, realizing that she was being childish. She hadn't come this far this fast on the corporate fast track to be derailed by a mere change in management.

She breathed deeply, steadying her nerves as she reached for the knob to the office of the new vice-president, Mary Melissa Mercy. It was Mercy who made Elvira the most uncomfortable. She just wasn't . . . right. And she was just *too* healthy. Unhealthily healthy. If there was such a thing.

Elvira paused at the door. There were voices coming from inside the office. Chanting.

It sounded to Elvira McGlone like some very weird aerobics class. Mary Melissa was calling out disjointed phrases, the others responding with even weirder mantras.

"The stomach is the center."

"Where life begins."

"No place in the afterlife."

"No place by God's side."

"The death of the stomach is the death of life."

"The homage to our God."

"The skeleton in the tree, symbolizing our strength and power."

"The burial of the innards."

"The Final Death."

The faddists must be talking shop again, Elvira decided.

When she pushed open the door to the room, Elvira McGlone discovered that these Three-G staffers weren't as strict with their vegetarianism as she had been led to understand.

The Three-G staff was arrayed around a long conference table. And they were not alone. They had been joined by several of the day's plant visitors.

These latter were not seated around the table, but splayed out on top of it.

Half of the tourists had been stripped of their skin, and their pulpy red subcutaneous flesh oozed blood. The rest were in the process of being eviscerated by members of the Three-G staff. Bloody strings of internal organs were being dragged from freshly gouged openings in the visitors' bellies. Hearts feebly pumped their last into small silver goblets. Some of the carcasses were being hauled out the broken window of Mary Melissa Mercy's office and into the garden beyond.

The pine floor was awash with blood. It was spilling from the drunkenly tilted silver goblets lifted to blood-smeared mouths.

The Vegans were actually drinking blood!

Elvira McGlone's mouth fell open, uncomprehending. A few Three-G staff members glanced up at her, their hands and faces streaked with red, their eyes hungry and animallike.

At the center, surveying all, Mary Melissa Mercy sat quietly on her desk, her clothes immaculate, her manner that of the calmest CEO. She, too, looked over at Elvira McGlone.

Elvira's brian worked furiously, trying to sort out the horrors her eyes beheld and at the same time determine some way to save herself from the fate of the pathetic half-human corpses littering her superior's office. If business school had taught Elvira McGlone anything at all, it was how to think on her feet.

"Oh, dear," she said, a sort of quavering earnestness in her voice. "If this is a bad time for you, I can come back later."

She grabbed for the doorknob to pull the door shut.

18

Grimly, Harold W. Smith led Remo into the security wing of Folcroft.

Entry into this area of the sanitarium was severely restricted. Medical staff were required to obtain special clearance before passing through the double-locked steel doors. Dr. Smith reviewed all applicants personally.

"Yes," Smith was saying, "this food-product tampering does bear a remarkable resemblance to events fifteen years ago. But as for the Leader's involvement, I believe Chiun is mistaken. It must be someone else. Perhaps the Leader had an ally or protégé?"

Remo shook his head. "Chiun is positive it's the Leader," he said firmly. "End of story."

"Er, yes," said Smith, unconvinced. "I only wish you had informed me of your progress. We could have coordinated. The loss of Don Pietro is most regrettable."

Remo glared at Smith. "Would you be happier if I'd gotten zapped, too?"

"I might have come up with some alternative," Smith said.

"Give it a rest, Smitty," Remo growled. "We

were on the damned assignment before you put
the key in the ignition."

Stung, Smith reached down to buckle his belt.
The movement brought a fresh wave of pain to
his stomach, and he turned his head to conceal
his grimace from Remo.

"Something wrong, Smitty?" Remo asked
suddenly.

"Ulcer," Smith said quickly.

"Try milk."

"The local dairy raised the price a nickel."

"Then die, if saving a freaking nickel's worth
that much to you," Remo growled.

The first door to the right along the two-tone
green corridor was closed, but as they passed it,
Remo peered through the window. Beyond the
wire-mesh double pane of glass he saw a wasted
blond figure covered by a thin white sheet. Jere-
miah Purcell. Better known as "the Dutchman."
The pupil of Chiun's first student, Nuihc. Now a
cataleptic vegetable. Another ghost from Remo's
past.

"One less fish in the sea," Remo said.

"That one will never bother us again," Smith
said flatly.

"I've heard that line before."

They passed on, Remo's expression tight and
worried.

"The Leader is in the next room," Smith said.

The CURE director pushed the thick steel
door open and stepped into the darkened room.

There was only one bed inside. It was positioned against a side wall, beneath a large picture window. The venetian blinds were drawn
over the window, obscuring the bars and the
thirty-foot drop to the ground below. Only a hint

of sunlight shone in through the overlapping white slats.

An ancient figure, like a honey-encrusted mummy, lay quietly in the bed. Assorted life-support equipment hummed and beeped around him, like mechanical spiders sucking the juices from the dry husk that was the patient through a profusion of intravenous tubes.

"The bills at Houston General Hospital became exorbitant," Smith explained. For some reason, he felt compelled to whisper. "Two years ago they went completely through the roof. It was an economic decision to move the Leader here. Nothing more."

"With you it always is, Smitty," Remo said. He examined the old man in the bed, moving the head to one side to look for the scar behind the right ear inflicted when Remo had shaved the *gyonshi*'s brain years before.

"This isn't the Leader," he said suddenly.

Smith seemed stunned. *"What?"* he asked, clutching at his rimless glasses as if they could offer some support.

"It isn't him!" Remo repeated hotly. "They pulled a switch on you! There's no scar behind the ear!"

Smith was shaking his gray-haired head. "Impossible!"

He leaned over to study the face of the man in the bed.

Obviously he was quite old. And he had distinctively Oriental features: the Mongoloid eye fold, the hairless chin, small nose. Unquestionably Chinese.

The patient's hands had been positioned peacefully, like those of a corpse, on his pigeon chest. They were gnarled and wrinkled. The index

finger had the same guillotine-shaped fingernail
Remo had described to Smith years ago. Smith
had ordered it removed when the patient was
first brought to Folcroft, but it proved too strong
for the sturdiest set of clippers. The staff had
finally just left it alone.

Smith stared closer at the nail. He thought
he had detected something. Something that
shouldn't have been there.

There! A twitch . . .

"Odd," Smith muttered. "There shouldn't be
any movement at all." He leaned closer, curious.

"Smitty! Get back!"

Remo leapt forward. Too late. The nail was in
Harold Smith's throat before the CURE director
had a chance to process his surprise.

The sharpened nail withdrew. As Smith lurched
to one side, Remo caught him and pulled him
away from the stirring figure on the bed. A
trickle of blood slid down the length of Smith's
narrow throat and seeped into the cheap fabric
of his shirt collar. Remo set Smith in a chair
near the bed, as the patient's eyes opened. The
desiccated head rose slightly from the pillow,
only to quiver and fall back, as if having ex-
hausted its last bit of strength.

"You have failed, *gweilo*," the patient wheezed
through a feeding tube. "Prepare you for your
Final Death." The old man's hand shot toward
his own throat, eager to end his existence. His
fingers were fast for a man his age, but Remo's
were faster.

Remo caught the hand while it was still a
foot away from reaching its mark. It quivered in
the air, as the old man attempted to comprehend
why he had failed. When he saw Remo's hand
curled around his own bony wrist it was as if he

were seeing a hand for the first time, and it was something frightening and alien. A look of terror crossed his emaciated features, and he attempted to force his throat forward into his frozen hand. His stringy neck trembled with the effort. His old eyes seemed unaware of Remo's index finger on his forehead, casually holding him down.

The *gyonshi* looked up uncomprehendingly, glancing left and then right, finally settling on Remo's angry features. "We are of the undead," his dry lips intoned. "The undead fear not the Masters of Sinanju."

"Yeah?" Remo said harshly. "Let's see if the undead feel pain." His fingers stabbed into the old man's side.

The puckered eyelids shot wide in shock. The orbs beneath were bloodshot and yellowed. The old man howled in pain like a skewered rat.

"I'll take that as a yes," Remo said. "Where is the Leader?"

"Consigning the stomach-desecrators to the Final Death," the old *gyonshi* wheezed, his mushroom-colored tongue stabbing desperately at the room's claustrophobic air.

"Not specific enough." Remo's hand dug in deeper. Not enough to shock the system and kill the old man, but enough to induce pain such as he had never before experienced. "Where?" Remo asked again.

"I do not know!" the man shouted, his back arching in pain.

Remo could see the old Chinese was telling the truth. He decided to try a different tack. "How did you get here?" he demanded.

"In my previous living death, I was a patient at the Houston hospital," the other rasped. "The

Leader's nurse came to me. The nurse helped me to become one with the Creed."

"The nurse?" Remo asked. "She's the one who infected you?"

The old man seemed puzzled. "Infected?" he asked.

"With her fingernail," Remo said.

"Infected," the old man chortled mockingly. "You blind fool!" His tone changed as Remo burrowed his hand in more deeply. The man sucked in a gulp of air over his blackened teeth. "She opened my mind to truths that will soon be understood by you as well, *gweilo*," he gasped.

"Who was this nurse?" Remo asked.

The old man's eyes circled the room one final time and locked on Remo's. They had the same strange, distant look as those of the other *gyonshi*.

"Mary Melissa Mercy was her blessed name," he rasped.

Remo asked, "Young? Super-healthy? Hair like a bonfire? Sensible white shoes?"

The old Chinese nodded. "She is responsible for placing me here in the Leader's stead. An honor I will cherish until the day I live in death." The old man seemed tired from his effort. His breathing had become a rattle.

Remo understood now. Mary Melissa Mercy. The woman from the Three-G health food company. The Leader had been there the whole time. And Chiun had known it. That's why he had led Remo away. It all made sense now, right down to the sensible shoes.

Remo looked down at the Chinese. "This is your lucky day," he said fiercely. "You get to die a second time."

He pressed the heel of his hand to the old

man's throat, until he felt the fragile windpipe collapse under his viselike grip. The rheumy eyes bulged one final time, then the old man's head lolled to one side.

Remo looked around the room for something to use to cut the man's throat.

He found nothing. The room was spartan, even by Folcroft standards. There wasn't even a nightstand near the bed. An unnecessary luxury, it seemed, for a man who presumably had been a mere shell on life-support.

"Dammit!"

Time was pressing. Smith would need medical attention, even though Remo knew there would be little that could be done for him. If Chiun hadn't been able to resist the *gyonshi* toxin, then an ordinary man like Smith would be no match for it.

He would have left the *gyonshi* as he was but for Chiun. The Master of Sinanju had seen some special significance in the release of the weird orange smoke, so Remo, while not entirely understanding it, decided he would honor the ritual.

He'd find a scalpel or something in the medical wing of the facility. But for now he turned his attention back to Harold Smith.

He didn't know how badly Smith had been affected by the *gyonshi* poison. The CURE director seemed to be sleeping peacefully at the moment. He remained slumped in the chair where Remo had left him, his chin pressed down against his chest, breathing deeply. In fact, he looked as relaxed as if he had been embalmed.

Remo experienced a moment of unreality. Chiun stricken. Now Smith. It felt like the walls were closing in.

He recalled the tale Chiun had told him years ago, when a Master of Sinanju—Remo suddenly remembered his name had been Pak—had encountered the blood-drinking *gyonshi* in a Shanghai forest. There, the House of Sinanju had nearly been rendered extinct, as one by one Pak's servants' relatives were overcome by a mist that took the form of men with long, killing nails. Only by deceit and cunning had Pak compelled the bloodsuckers to spare him.

Now, untold generations later, Remo stood in Pak's sandals. And he found them cold.

Remo shook off his fear.

He decided to get Smith to a doctor, then return later to release the bad air of the dead man.

Remo stepped up to the chair and slipped his left hand behind Smith's stiff neck. His right found the backs of his employer's knees, and he started to gather the old man up.

At the moment of Remo Williams' maximum exposure, Harold Smith's eyes sprang open in a wild burst of energy. Remo felt the vibrations as Smith's heart rate increased almost fivefold.

Smith's hand shot up in a stunningly quick strike.

There was little time to react. Remo felt the sudden, unstoppable jab to his throat. His blood ran cold.

Remo Williams was spared only by the fact that Harold W. Smith was by nature a meticulously neat individual.

The older man's fingernails were always kept clipped and filed precisely. There were no sharp edges to pierce the skin. The blunt tip of his index finger merely poked the flesh of Remo's neck, like a soft eraser.

"Nice try," Remo snapped, dropping Smith back into the chair. A cold sweat trickled down the gully of Remo's back.

Hot-eyed, Smith tried again. This time, by holding his finger to Remo's throat and digging at his carotid artery, leaving only pale tracks that quickly faded.

Firmly, Remo removed Smith's hand and forced it into a harmless fist. Smith looked up, but the gray eyes that stared into Remo's were not those of Harold W. Smith. They were those of Don Pietro. Of the old *gyonshi* in the bed behind him. Of the Chinese couple. Of Sal Mondello. Of the black-clad Oriental with the creepy eyebrow who had ambushed Chiun.

They were the eyes of the Leader. The Leader who stared mockingly into Remo's soul through the vacant, dispossessed eyes of his superior.

And a voice that was unlike Smith's began to chant.

"The stomach is the center. The house of all life and death. Life begins and ends here. The soul dwells there. Destroy the stomach and destroy all life. We are the holy saviors of the stomach. We wander the earth as the undead, slaves to our God, punishers of all transgressors."

"Tell it to the head psychologist," Remo said bitterly, hefting Smith carefully into his arms.

He carried him out of the hospital room, knowing that his employer was as lost to him as the Master of Sinanju.

For there was no cure for *gyonshism*—except by slitting the throat and releasing the orange smoke that clogged Smith's lungs.

Remo knew he might have to perform that operation on Smith. And he would do it.

But who would free the Master of Sinanju

from his living hell? For Remo knew he could never bring himself to cut the throat of the man who was more than a father to him—not even if Chiun himself were to beg for such a boon.

19

Mary Melissa Mercy stood before the Leader in the security room at Three-G, Incorporated, the room he had been using as his headquarters. He was seated before a bank of television monitors.

"The Master of Sinanju has succumbed!" she trumpeted proudly.

The words thrilled him. So many years . . . so much wasted time . . . so hungry for vengeance. Now, fulfilled.

"He is dead?" the Leader asked eagerly.

"Better." The girl's tone seemed to shimmer with delight. "He has become one with the holy Creed. He is *gyonshi* now."

The Leader nodded. "The Taoist," he said, knowingly.

"Yes, Leader."

"The last any would suspect. Our bitterest enemy, but for Sinanju. The Shanghai Web proved true. The Master and his *gweilo* thought they had evaded each snare laid in their path. They did not dream that only through flight could they escape their doom. Only through flight."

His hands grasped the arms of the old-fashioned wooden chair that now served as his

throne. He had once had a true throne of rose-
wood and rare gems, but Sinanju had robbed him
of that glory. Just as they had robbed him of
fifteen years of his life in death. The Final
Death. But now his long years of shame had been
expunged by the words of his *gweilo* nurse.

"The plan?" he asked, his blind pearl eyes upturned to where he sensed the girl to be.

The girl hesitated. "All is not well," she
admitted.

A frown like a spring thundercloud passed
across the Leader's shriveled purple features.
"Explain."

"Their dead number only in the thousands,
Leader. Not millions. Your requirements for
the Final Death have not been achieved." She
shrugged. "Not enough chicken-eaters, I guess."

The Leader seemed to relax ever-so-slightly.
"The despised Master of Sinanju is no more?"
he asked.

"Yes, Leader."

"If the Master can be stopped, cannot the
pupil?"

Mary frowned. "Yes," she replied at length.

"Then where is the failure?"

"The failure is to your ancestors, Leader. To
our Creed."

"Missy, this Creed of which you speak is as
old as I, and older still. It is no more yours than
the air you breathe, or the ground upon which
you tread. The *gyonshi* will survive Sinanju, that
is all that matters. Be it by a week, a day, an
hour. The *gweilo* will come, and he will be consumed. Like the sacred blood that breaks our
fast."

"But . . . the Final Death?"

"Will be achieved, Missy. There are other poisons. Plagues, famines, disease. If I am not here to carry out the work, it will be another. It will be you." He said it as an offhanded gesture. She was, after all, but a woman. And a white. She could be true to the Creed in spirit, but not in blood.

Mary Melissa Mercy's ample chest swelled with pride. "I will not let you down, O Leader."

He turned away from her, waving his guillotine-nailed hand in a shooing gesture. "I know you will not, my nurse."

20

The Master of Sinanju knew not where he abided.

Upon regaining his senses, Chiun muttered a low curse for having allowed himself to fall victim to the Leader's trap.

The Leader knew what Chiun would do. Knew what he must do. It was the Leader himself who, years before, had infected the Sinanju elder with the *gyonshi* virus. The Leader knew of Chiun's father. It had been the Leader who had engineered his father's ultimate disgrace. If the elder of the village had succeeded in striking Chiun so many years ago, his plan would have come to fruition that much sooner. Sinanju would have ended then, the long bloodline severed.

But Sinanju had not ended. It lived. It lived in Chiun. It now lived in Remo as well.

Chiun got out of bed, setting his sandaled feet to the floor.

The Master of Sinanju glanced down at his feet. Most curious. It was unusual that the American doctors had not removed his sandals.

Chiun studied the room carefully. The walls were painted in two unappetizing shades of green. Folcroft. He did not know how he had

gotten here. He hoped that someone other than
Remo had found him with the Taoist. Remo
would never allow him to live down the shame
of letting a Chinaman land a blow, even if that
Chinese had been a *gyonshi* bloodsucker. It would
be just like Remo to overlook an important detail
such as that.

The green room seemed smaller now. Much
smaller. Only a quarter of the size it had been a
moment before.

It must be the *gyonshi* poison, affecting my
senses, the Master of Sinanju decided.

Chiun felt his neck. His hand came away in
horror. Blood. His fingertips were coated in
blood. There was a gash in his neck as wide
around as a Sumerian gold piece.

It was strange his body had not gone to work to
heal the wound. Stranger still that the American
doctors who seemed to sprout up like dandelions
around the Fortress Folcroft of Emperor Smith
had not bound his neck in thick sheets of
disease-ridden bandages. That always seemed to
be their answer to everything.

The room now appeared smaller still.

Chiun pressed his hand to his forehead. Beads
of perspiration had formed there. They mingled
with the drying blood and rolled onto his palm.
He closed his hand delicately around them.

Something was wrong. A Master of Sinanju
does not perspire without cause.

The walls continued to close in.

It could not be mechanical, this closing inward. The Master of Sinanju felt no vibration of
gears grinding. He did not discern the walls
moving toward him. Yet they were close enough
that he could have reached out and touched
them with his bloodstained fingers.

If this was some diabolic trap, whoever had engineered it had forgotten one thing.

He had forgotten to close the only door.

The Master of Sinanju padded out into the hallway. He was free.

When he looked back into the room, the walls had returned to the positions they had occupied when he first opened his eyes.

Chiun nodded to himself. There was no doubt now. The Leader's poison. It was the only explanation. His mind was playing tricks on him. It would cleanse itself soon enough.

The hallway was cast in a deep gloom. There were no lights on, and beyond the windows it was dark. Chiun did not know where such sparse light as there was originated.

He sharpened his senses. There was no one else nearby. He expanded his awareness. The entire building was empty.

At the end of the hall was a long wooden staircase. Padding to the top step, he descended this to the ground floor.

The stairs creaked beneath his feet.

That should not be. He was a Master of Sinanju.

Taking a sip of reviving air, Chiun took a cautious step. Still, the stair creaked in complaint. And it seemed as if there were more of them now. They stretched limitlessly into some infinite abyss below.

Something was desperately wrong. He continued, humiliation burning with every betraying creak.

Chiun touched his neck once more. The wound was as fresh as the moment it had been opened. It felt larger now. Even his neck felt larger. As if it too were growing to accommodate the expanding injury.

Suddenly, the stairs ended and Chiun found himself standing at the sterile entrance to Folcroft Sanitarium. The door was open, and the chill air of night blew in around Chiun's ankles.

He looked back. It was no longer the staircase behind him, but the door to Folcroft. Somehow he had ended up outside, beyond the door, and the door was closed.

He was being taunted. Tested.

But he did not fear. Fear he had banished long ago.

The Master of Sinanju tucked his hands into the sleeves of his kimono and disappeared into the gathering dark, where owls stared and called their eternal question.

"His neural activity just went off the charts!"

Dr. Lance Drew studied the brain-wave monitor screen next to The Master of Sinanju's bed. On the screen a series of gently flowing waves had become a collection of sharp, almost vertical lines. They shot up, dropped down, and shot up again. Several disappeared off the top of the monitor, as if to escape their own frenetic energy.

A second doctor and three nurses had joined Dr. Drew at Chiun's bedside. Frantically, they pored over printouts and EKGs.

"What is it?" Remo asked anxiously. Smith lay docile where Remo had laid him, on the room's spare bed. Chiun's condition had gone critical just as Remo entered the room.

"I don't know," Dr. Drew said. "He was stable until just this minute. Now ..." He shook his head. "I don't know what it is." He noticed Smith's prone form for the first time.

"What's the matter with Dr. Smith?" he asked.

"Same thing that's wrong with him," Remo said, nodding to Chiun.

One of the attending physicians went to Smith, checked his vital signs, and said, "He'll keep."

"Then give me a hand here," the doctor said, shaking his head. "We're in for a rough night."

A crisp professional voice interjected itself. "Doctor . . ."

It was one of the nurses. Chiun's face had twitched slightly, then returned to its parchment calmness. It resembled a death mask.

The doctor examined the monitor. The lines continued to spike dangerously. "If this keeps up, we're going to lose him," the doctor warned, glancing up at his colleagues. "He could burn out his entire nervous system."

Remo stood helplessly at Chiun's bedside. One of the nurses attempted to shepherd him to one side, but it was like pushing smoke. Each time he somehow shifted away without, apparently, moving his feet. She spoke gently of the need to give the physicians room to work. Two thick-wristed hands grasped hers and clapped them together. Not hard. But she couldn't separate her palms afterward.

She hurried off to her jeweler. Surely he would know how to un-weld her wedding ring from the one on her right ring finger.

"His heart rate's increased," the other doctor was saying.

"Respiration, too."

Remo hovered over Chiun's bedside, a spectator to a battle he could barely understand. The

Master of Sinanju's life hung in the balance. Now Smith's as well. He'd probably be next.

"If only we knew what kind of infection we're dealing with," the doctor lamented at one point, "we'd have something to go on."

"It's Chinese," Remo said.

"Can you do better than that?" Dr. Drew demanded, not looking up.

"No," Remo admitted. What could he tell them that would help? They wouldn't believe the truth. And if they did, so what? Vampirism had no cure. Its victims were neither dead nor alive.

Remo's anxious eyes went to his mentor's face.

The Master of Sinanju was peaceful in repose. It was as if the medical team had forgotten there was a patient in the room, so busy were they monitoring their equipment. Languishing amid this nest of high-tech machinery, surrounded by white-clad Folcroft doctors and nurses, Chiun looked old and frail.

His face twitched spasmodically once again, then settled back into its normal pattern.

"If this is good-bye, Little Father," Remo said softly, "I swear no *gyonshi* will celebrate this day."

"What's that?" Dr. Drew asked distractedly. No answer. He looked up to see the door swinging shut behind Remo's resolute back.

After Remo had gone, Harold W. Smith sat up stiffly in bed. The pain in his stomach and throat were gone, although there was a slight tightening in his chest.

"Dr. Smith!" Dr. Drew exclaimed. "Please do not exert yourself! We will get to you in a moment!"

"Nonsense," Smith croaked, tightening the knot of his Dartmouth tie. "I feel fine."

"But the young man who brought you in here . . ."

"Do not concern yourself," he insisted, waving his hand in dismissal. "He is too prone to worry. I feel fine. Now if you will excuse me, I have a telephone call to make." He slid from the bed and stepped briskly from the room.

One of the nurses cocked an eyebrow. "Did he sound strange to you?" she asked the others.

"He always sounds strange," said the other nurse.

"Actually, that was the first time he ever sounded normal to me," said Dr. Drew. "And I've been on staff ten years."

"Why do you suppose he kept rubbing his fingernail?" the first nurse whispered to the second, as they resumed ministering to the old Korean.

He did not know why he had come here. He only knew that he had felt compelled to do so.

The night air was heavy with moisture. The dampness clung to his kimono. The dew on the freshly mowed grass collected in dollops on the tops of his feet.

Long Island Sound stretched out into infinity behind the sanitarium. No boats bobbed on its surface. No lights were visible. No starlight reflected in the lapping waves. The Sound was totally black, like spilled crude.

Chiun, Master of Sinanju, peered into the distance. Not totally black after all, he saw now.

Wallowing somewhere on the far horizon, there was a grayness. It swirled there for a moment in eternity and then shot out to either side, spreading outward from that single finite point until it had become great gray wings.

Wings which began to beat remorselessly toward shore, spreading and widening.

They became a tidal wave, covering the vast distance to the shore in mere seconds.

The gray wings of fog enveloped Chiun's legs, rolling in around him in thick currents, but not stirring the wispy hair clinging to his venerable chin and in puffs over his alert ears.

It moved across the shore, obscuring the huge building behind Chiun.

Soon there was nothing but fog all around. No sky, no ground, no sea. Just the fog.

And there was a blackness in it. Like an evil pit in a rotted peach. It was vague and indistinguishable one moment, solid the next. It leaped around Chiun in the protective haze of the swirling gray fog.

Chiun followed its movements impassively.

The black fog-within-the-fog split in two, then the two vaporous shapes became four, and the four, eight. They spun kaleidoscopic patterns around him, encroaching, then retreating, bold and timid by turns.

Chiun paid them no heed. He stared resolutely out to where the horizon had been.

"Sinanjuuuuu . . ." The word was a taunt.

Chiun ignored the voice.

There was no breeze, and there were no other sounds or smells. Chiun was not even certain if he stood on solid ground any longer. There was just the dampness of the fog against his face. And the circling black mist.

"Do you invite us in?" A chorus of voices this time.

Chiun remained fixated on a long-vanished point in space, refusing to answer.

"You are frightened," scoffed a single voice.

"He has much to fear," another agreed.

"Much indeed," a third chimed in. "For he remembers Shanghai."

Chiun spoke. "I fear not *gyonshi* vermin." He refused to focus on the mist.

"Then invite us in," the first voice dared.

"Invite us in now, Sinanju Master."

"It is an invitation to death," Chiun said blankly.

The black mist circled closer. "Do you fear death, O great Master of Sinanju?" the voice whispered mockingly in his ear.

Chiun's eyes remained shards of flint. "I was not referring to my own death, *gyonshi* mist." Chiun delicately removed his hands from his kimono sleeves. He intertwined his fingers before him so that they formed a yellow basket of bones.

In his heart, he prepared himself.

"You are invited in," he said softly.

The tightness in his chest had worsened.

The man Smith had been would have been concerned, but not overly so. He would have assumed that it was simple esophageal reflux, or his ulcer acting up again. Were it to persist, he would have had it checked in a few days.

The thing that Harold W. Smith had become, however, did not care at all. Smith was a mere vessel now. The latest adherent of an ancient Creed. An expendable extension of the Leader.

But this thing that inhabited the body of Harold W. Smith was also in possession of Smith's knowledge.

Although Smith did not fully understand all that was happening to him, the thing did.

The Leader was of the Creed, he knew. The Leader had helped what had once been Harold W. Smith to be reborn in death. The Leader was all-knowing. The Leader could explain his new purpose to Smith the Undead.

But the Leader was in danger.

This "Remo" was a threat to the Leader, who Remo believed dwelled in the Three-G, Incorporated, health food company in Woodstock, New York. He was on his way now.

Smith's secretary was not at her desk when the Smith-vessel stumbled toward its office. For some reason, the body was not fully responding to the commands issued by its brain.

It wanted to stand erect, but the body was hunched. It clutched at its chest, trying to hold the pain in. In this doubled-over manner, the Smith-thing crossed the office and dropped into the cracked-leather chair behind the desk.

It was an effort to call up a phone directory for upstate New York over the computer terminal, and secure the number. But this was done.

When the phone was finally answered, the pains in the Smith-vessel's chest had grown sharper and more localized. It began to sweat. The sweat was cold, clammy.

The breath came with difficulty. His left arm grew numb.

"You . . . must . . . must . . . warn . . . Leader," the Smith-thing wheezed into the phone receiver. "Remo . . . Sinanju . . . coming . . . uuuhhhh . . ."

The receiver dropped to the floor as the Smith-thing slumped forward onto the sparse wooden desk, clutching his left breast as if a stake had been driven through his ribs and into his heart.

*   *   *

In her Woodstock office, Mary Melissa Mercy delicately returned the receiver to its cradle and hurried off to inform the Leader that the Shanghai Web had snared another foe.

All that remained now was the hated *gweilo*.

21

Mary Melissa Mercy knew at an early age that she would devote her life to nursing the sick. As far back as she could remember she had practiced her art. Bandaging the family dog. Listening to family hearts with a stethoscope fashioned from a Dixie cup and plastic hosing. Once, she had even tried to "inoculate" a neighborhood playmate with a rusty nail—which resulted in a severe case of tetanus.

Mary Melissa got to visit the playmate in the hospital, thus opening up an entire new world to her young imagination. A world that smelled disinfectant-clean.

As soon as she had graduated from high school, Mary Melissa Mercy enrolled in the Lone Star Nursing School. It was a dream come true. And why shouldn't it have been? If there was one thing Mary Melissa cared about, it was health.

She had never been sick a day in her life. When every other kid was suffering from colds and flu and measles and chicken pox, Mary Melissa was always in the pink of health. Even a case of the sniffles would have been unusual for Mary Melissa Mercy.

She attributed her remarkable good health to one thing and one thing alone: vegetarianism.

If nursing was Mary Melissa Mercy's vocation, then vegetarianism was her avocation.

It wasn't something she had to do in order to maintain her perfect figure. It wasn't something she thought she'd try because her peers did it. They were beef eaters. It wasn't something that had been forced on her by her parents.

It was because Mary Melissa Mercy couldn't stand the taste of blood.

Little did she realize that her twin passions and single phobia would collide mere weeks after graduating from the Lone Star Nursing School, in a small, poorly ventilated corner room in the terminal ward of Houston General Hospital.

The elderly patient in Room 334 was enshrouded in mystery. He was known to the staff as Mr. Nichols, which everyone agreed couldn't be his name, for he was unmistakably Chinese.

The old Chinese had been left at the hospital many years before by his grandson, a Remo Nichols. This young man had dropped twenty-five thousand dollars in cash to pay for the life-support systems, and quickly vanished. Before the money had run out more began coming in, to cover the spiraling cost of sustaining the old Chinese gentleman, but the grandson never returned to visit his comatose grandfather.

Mary Melissa thought that was disgraceful. The old man had been left there to waste away by a relative who had no intention of ever returning.

She took on that patient as a personal cause.

At first, Mary Melissa told herself she gave the man special attention only because of his personal situation. That was all. But in fact, as with everything else in her life, she had become obsessive about him.

She had been obsessive in her quest to become a nurse, obsessive in her strict adherence to vegetarian dogma, and now she was obsessive in her care of the terminally ill Chinese gentleman.

And the trigger for that obsessiveness was the fingernail. It couldn't have been anything else.

What is its purpose? Mary Melissa often wondered, as she trimmed the old man's hair and sponged his flaking, purplish skin.

She had tried at one point to trim the sharpened guillotine tip of the index fingernail, but it just would not cut. She even jutted the tip of her pink tongue through her pearl-perfect teeth and scrunched up her freckled forehead in determination as she bore down on the nail with all her might, but all she succeeded in doing was snapping her clippers. The nail remained smooth and shiny.

Mary Melissa would sit for hours, eating salads from the cafeteria and holding one-sided conversations with the old man, because she had read that even the comatose were sometimes cognizant of their surroundings. And who knew? Maybe she could talk him back to health.

Mary Melissa Mercy believed in miracles.

The nursing staff at Houston General thought she was as loopy as mating squid, but no one complained, because Mary Melissa Mercy was the only nurse who undertook the distasteful job of veggie-grooming without complaint.

One day, a miracle seemed to occur.

Over the rhythmic sounds of the ventilator that assisted the man's breathing, she heard a sound issue from parted purplish lips.

"Missy . . ."

"My name! You spoke my name! You can hear!"

"Missy . . ."

"I've gotten through to you!"

Later, Mary Melissa Mercy tried to explain her progress to the attending physician. He was a cynic.

"Nurse Mercy," he had said. "I know you're excited. But try to listen carefully. The patient is brain-damaged. He will never regain consciousness. He will never leave that bed, except for the county morgue."

"But he said my name! He called me Missy! Missy was my childhood nickname!"

"Missy," the doctor patiently explained, "is a very Chinese form of address when speaking to a young woman. I would not take any such vocalization seriously."

But Mary Melissa Mercy did take the patient's words seriously. In the weeks that followed, she devoted herself to the old Chinese.

She knew on an instinctual level that he realized she was in the room with him. She spoke to him for hours on end. About the weather. About current events. About her life—which consisted mainly of the same twelve-by-fifteen foot room the old man lived in.

Her ministrations were rewarded one late afternoon, with the flicker of a translucent eyelid.

Many in her profession would have disregarded such an event. They would have called it an example of "unfocused neural impulses," or something equally random, and gone on ignoring the old man.

But Mary Melissa Mercy had seen it. Seen it with her own two eyes.

Over the next few weeks there were more

such twitches. Mostly around the eyes, but some were located in the hand. The one with the strange super-hard nail.

Mary Melissa was changing the old man's linen one day when his eyes snapped open completely. They were hideous. Like twin fungi. She did not back away in fear as some might have but moved closer to him, peering down into his dark, drawn face.

Mary Melissa Mercy had thought those eyes hadn't seen the light of day in more than six years, but the sight of them told her it had been much longer than that. They were so white, it was difficult for her to discern any pupil at all. She finally gave up trying. It didn't matter, however. He could see. Perhaps more clearly than a sighted man. Those blind, milky eyes bored into her very soul.

He forced two words from between thin lips.

"Reject . . . meat."

"Yes, yes!" Mary Melissa cried, thinking the patient had absorbed her lectures on proper Vegan diet.

As quickly as they had opened, the milky eyes closed again. The old man seemed tired from his effort. His eyes rolled and locked beneath their parchment lids. The twitching stopped for several days afterward, as he regained what little strength he had.

Mary Melissa Mercy told no one of the miracle she had wrought.

Over the course of the next year, the old man's strength increased. He seemed to possess a boundless determination to recover. It appeared to Mary Melissa that, even in his obviously advanced years, the old man had some overriding reason to cling to life. A drive. Something that compelled him to beat almost insurmountable odds to recover.

In the second month after that first time his eyes had opened, the old man began to speak in complete sentences. The words seemed to be Chinese. The voice struggled laboriously over the pronunciation, as the vocal chords vibrated for the first time in over a decade. A few English syllables seemed to pepper the subvocal murmurings.

The head would sway from side to side—that started shortly after he had begun opening his eyes—and he would wheeze out a stream of unintelligible nonsense.

The words he said most often sounded like "sin and chew." They seemed to trouble the old man greatly. Often the phrase would seem a curse; at times it was said almost reverentially, and at others, as a plea.

Mary Melissa was so interested in the old man that she went to the public library to try to find out what had caused him so much mental anguish. It took some doing, but finally she found it.

It was Sinanju—just some tiny little fishing village in Communist North Korea, nestled in the heavily industrialized western coastline. It didn't even appear on most maps, it was so small. Mr. Nichols had probably spent some time there as a boy, she decided.

Like most Americans, Mary Melissa Mercy lumped the entire Asian continent into one big neighborhood.

The old man became more animated as time wore on. He also became consciously aware of Mary Melissa's presence. Eventually, he told her in his halting English that he had learned the language thanks to her and her hours of disconnected ramblings. He told her that, despite appearances, they were much alike.

"Really?" she asked.

"We do not soil our stomachs with the flesh of animals."

"How did you know I was a vegetarian?"

"We are one Creed, you and I, Missy," rasped the Chinese named Nichols. "Soul mates. Connected in mind and spirit."

A one-sided relationship, akin to idol worship, began to develop between the old man in Room 334 and Mary Melissa Mercy.

Then the bottom fell out. Orders were passed into the terminal ward saying that the old man was to be moved out of the hospitial at the end of the month. When Mary Melissa Mercy tried to find out where, she was told the new location was not known.

In tears, she ran to tell the poor old man of his fate.

He was sitting up in bed, propped against a half-dozen pillows. The blinds were opened wide and he was basking in the midday sun, which made his scaly skin appear livid and strange.

"Sir," Mary Melissa had said, sobbing. "They are taking you from me."

He smiled thinly—a corpse's grimace. "Taking me where?" he asked.

"I don't know," Mary Melissa answered. "I guess it must be your grandson's doing."

"Grandson?" he asked. His purple head still moved from side to side, like that of a cobra weaving to unseen music.

Mary Melissa had never mentioned the ungrateful youth to Mr. Nichols before. She had hoped to spare him the grief.

"Yes," she admitted. "He brought you here years ago. He has paid for you to stay here all these years," she added brightly, as if to sugar-coat the familial ingratitude.

The smile vanished. "Missy," he said coldly, "the grandson of whom you speak is no grandson of mine."

Mary Melissa Mercy shrugged—a wasted gesture. "I know, but what are you going to do with family?" She tried to joke, but her heart was breaking. In truth, she felt closer to the old Chinese man lying in that hospital bed than she did to her own kin. They all ate meat and drank the blood, which they called "juice."

"This 'grandson' is Sinanju," he spat. It was the first time she had heard him use that word since regaining full consciousness.

"He's from Korea?" Mary Melissa had asked. She was puzzled. A doctor had once told her that the man who dropped the old Chinese gentleman off had been Caucasian.

The old man beckoned Mary Melissa Mercy closer. His breathing was labored. She had grown used to his rank breath more than a year before. "He is not what he appears, this *gweilo*," he said. "He is servant to an ancient evil, as is his master. Both must be stopped."

Mary Melissa Mercy felt a strange tingling sensation in the pit of her stomach. There was something otherworldly about this elderly Chinese as he stared blankly up at her. There was something in those eyes that held the key to her destiny. She just knew it.

"It is this *gweilo* who rendered me immobile," he said, "condemning me to a living death. You

will help me to stop him. You will help me to
end the line of Sinanju."

"I don't understand. I thought Sinanju was a
place."

"Sinanju is a cult of assassins. I am only one
of their many victims. They have warred with
my people for hundreds of years."

"Do they eat meat?" Mary Melissa asked
slowly.

"They are duck-eaters."

"Then I hate them. I had baby ducks when I
was eight."

Mr. Nichols nodded weakly. "You will help
me to achieve the Final Death longed for by my
Creed."

This was it! This was why he had pulled himself back from the brink of death. A mission!
Mary Melissa could tell the old man was about
to impart some great wisdom to her. This was
why she had stayed so long. This was why she
had found him so endlessly fascinating.

He brought his gnarled index finger into the
air. Sunlight reflected off of the tip of the razor-
sharp nail. It remained poised there, as if to as-
sist the old man in making some great oratorical
point. But no more words came.

The finger dropped, slicing into the side of
Mary Melissa Mercy's exposed neck in a delicate, almost loving gesture.

And her mind was opened to the universe.

Mary Melissa Mercy, *gyonshi*, obediently arranged the patient switch. She found another old
Chinese man to take her benefactor's place. He
was in the surgical wing for a gall bladder operation. It was easy enough to do. Practically no one

but Mary had been in Room 334 for almost three years. They would not recognize the difference.

She had wheeled Mr. Nichols—whom she now addressed as "the Leader"—to an access elevator in the surgical wing and out of the hospital.

She had stayed on at Houston General only long enough to shape and strengthen the nail of the imposter to match that of the Leader by applying a varnish made from an ancient recipe.

And then they had simply vanished.

It had taken several years for the Leader to regain his strength. Mary Melissa Mercy knew that he had recovered as much as his aged body would allow.

Several years to recreate the ancient poison. Several years for the Leader to perfect his scheme. Several years to engineer the downfall of Sinanju, a scheme which was approaching fruition at last.

And now, the evil Master of Sinanju had been defeated. They had been warned that his protégé, the *gweilo*, was en route. He would be defeated as well.

Mary Melissa Mercy didn't know who it was who had called her to tell her that Remo was on his way, and she didn't care. She suspected it was whomever employed Sinanju in America. There was no other person who could have had knowledge of Remo's next move. And that person had become *gyonshi* now, as well.

The afternoon wind blew a fragrant lilac aroma through the huge broken window of Mary Melissa's Three-G office. She hadn't bothered to have maintenance fix the window. Right now they were too interested in eviscerating rats in the boiler room to install a new pane anyway.

She stepped through the window and out into the lush garden.

The smell was stronger here, and she lifted her slender nose to the air and inhaled greedily. They were here. All around her. The sacrifices.

From every tree in the thick garden there hung a skeletal corpse. Strips of flesh still clung to ribs. Blood still dripped slowly and deliberately from dangling toes.

The ground had been freshly turned in splotchy patches throughout the garden. The buried internal organs spread widening stains of darkness around the earthy mounds.

This was the smell that Mary Melissa Mercy so loved. The smell of the unclean meat-eaters. The smell of death. It reminded her of her first hospital visit.

She was even getting used to the taste of blood finally. But only because she had been assured drinking blood was central to the practice of the *gyonshi* religion—which it was.

The Leader sat in a wheelchair in the middle of the main path. A plaid afghan was tucked neatly around his knees and his hands were cradled carefully in his lap. But for the array of corpses that swayed and rattled like bony wind chimes in the breeze around him, he would not have looked out of place on the porch of any rest home in America.

"The *gweilo* will be here soon, Leader," Mary Melissa Mercy said.

He looked up at her, his white eyes unblinking. He smiled evilly.

"We will be ready, Missy," he said softly. "The Shanghai Web demands one last victim. Vengeance shall be ours. The Final Death will achieve dominion over this tired world." He paused, as if to drink in a vision only his sightless eyes could perceive.

"And for our eternal enemies, the Ultimate Death . . ."

22

Night was falling on the longest day of Remo Williams' life.

He steered his rented car through the dying light, his face a mask of single-minded concentration.

Remo racked his brain, trying to remember all that Chiun had told him years before about the Chinese vampires, but the images were intertwined with flashes of other, more personal, memories.

He pushed these away.

The vampires cannot enter a residence unless invited, Remo recalled. He was pretty sure of that one. A lot of good that did him now. They were all over Three-G like glassy-eyed cockroaches. And they were as fast as Sinanju, but not as strong.

The first time Sinanju had encountered the *gyonshi* Creed had been in a forest near what would later become Shanghai, and they had asked the Master of the time if he would invite them in. Did that mean all Remo had to say was "no" and they'd leave him alone long enough to kill them? Who knew? It didn't seem reasonable, but neither did the idea of vegetarian vampires who drank blood.

They were shape-changers as well. Remo remembered that much of the legend. Would he find himself facing a *gyonshi* vampire one minute and a spitting cobra the next?

And they hid in mist, he recalled. Or maybe they became the mist itself. Remo wasn't certain which. The legends were vague.

All he could call up beyond that were images of bats and wooden stakes and garlic and castles—distortions of the reality that had given rise to the European vampire tradition.

His thoughts turned again to Chiun, lying alone, possibly dying, on that hospital bed back at Folcroft.

He was in this one alone, he knew.

Smith would be of no help. For all Remo knew, he had joined the rest of the vampires by now. At least Chiun had been saved that ignominy. His nervous system had given out well before the *gyonshi* virus could turn him into one of the undead.

Remo gripped the steering wheel of his rented car tightly and raced along the twisting mountain road. Woodstock lay ahead. And the hilly eminence that was Three-G Incorporated.

In the blink of an eye, on the shore that had no name because it did not belong to reality, the black mist congealed into human form.

The black-clad figure was sickly thin, with cadaverous features and pale, almost albino pigmentation.

The guillotine-shaped nail on its index finger shot forward toward Chiun's throat in a near perfect jab. Near perfect, however, was not good enough.

Chiun easily sidestepped the blow and fired

his elbow in a backward thrust, crushing the
windpipe and sending a font of blood squirting
from the stricken creature's mouth.

Its eyes wide open in surprise, the *gyonshi* fell.
The gray fog swirled around the body and accepted it. It congealed, squeezing like a vaporous
fist, and slowly vanished from sight.

Chiun wheeled. Two more of the shapes were
emerging from the mist behind him. They were
as pale as the first, their cheeks sunken, their
teeth clearly visible through the thin, almost
transparent facial skin. Both raised their hands
in the air, assuming a menacing posture.

Chiun took this as an invitation and sent both
fists rocketing into the sternums of the two creatures. They howled in pain as twin rivers of
blood erupted from their chests. They, too, retreated in the ever-thickening fog like skulking
dogs.

"We are shape-changers as well, Master of Sinanju," the first *gyonshi* voice whispered in his
ear. "Do you not fear us?"

"A Master of Sinanju fears nothing, Chinese
vermin," Chiun replied haughtily.

"No ... ?" the voice faded in the distance.
The remaining misty shapes vanished amid the
swirl of gray fog, leaving the Master of Sinanju
standing alone.

The fog continued to move in circular patterns
around him. It was as if his world were no bigger
than the nearest visible point, only five feet all
around him.

A sound fluttered somewhere in the swirling
vapor.

Chiun's hunting ears were alert to it immediately. It was a graceful glide. More akin to a ballet movement then a footfall.

Something about it was familiar. Almost . . .

A lone figure stepped from out of the fog. He wore a black business suit and tie. His face was flat and smooth. His features were not unlike those of Chiun as a young man. And although his stomach bled profusely, the vision that stood before Chiun did not seem to mind.

Chiun's eyes widened in disbelief. "Nuihc!" he hissed.

The younger man smiled. "You are looking well, Uncle."

And now the Master of Sinanju knew he stood face-to-face with his greatest pain—alone.

The first thing Remo noticed, on driving up the wide strip of asphalt that serviced Poulette Farms Poultry & Foods, Incorporated, was the unnatural quiet.

The second thing he noticed were the bodies.

The bodies were even quieter.

The building was surrounded on all four sides by an eight-foot-high hurricane fence. The fence ran parallel to the road and veered off along the property line.

Someone had snipped the chain link from its fastenings and rolled it up into two gigantic tubular coils at two corners of the fence. Suspended along the long, bare metal support bars were Poulette Farms employees, hanging by their feet like elongated pale-pink pigs in a Chinese butcher shop window.

And in the center of them all was Henry Poulette himself, surrounded by his omnipresent gaggle of secretaries. His gentle tufts of yellow hair blew softly in the mild mountain breeze.

The difference between the Henry Cackleberry Poulette of the moment and the Henry

Cackleberry Poulette of Poulette Farms' award-winning commercials was that in the commercials, Poulette's internal organs were tastefully tucked away in their proper body cavities under his well-tailored suit. Not buried in a mound of bloody dirt directly below his inverted head. Remo knew from past encounters what the mounds concealed.

Remo saw that all of Poulette's employees had suffered the same fate. Throats slit. Blood drained. Organs extracted and buried. It was some sort of combination of the Leader's vampire Creed and the ultimate vegetarian revenge.

Remo drove past the still, upended bodies toward the glistening patch of glass in the hills above.

It was time for the final showdown between Sinanju and the *gyonshi.*

"Behold your handiwork, Uncle," Nuihc proclaimed. He spread his hands wide. The raw wound in his stomach continued to pour blood into the cloud below him. Chiun saw that Nuihc's feet were invisible in the half-foot-thick blanket of fog. He maintained a pensive silence.

"Not the best stroke available to you," Nuihc continued, indicating his own stomach. "But one that effectively took me by surprise. Still, it is rather unlike you, Uncle. You are usually more tidy than this."

Chiun's face had become impassive. He stared silently beyond Nuihc, his expression carved from alabaster. He was remembering a time from many years ago. Nuihc had wrested control of the village of Sinanju from Chiun, usurping the title of Reigning Master. Remo, wounded, virtually helpless, had entered into mortal combat on

Chiun's behalf. For the Master of Sinanju was forbidden to harm a fellow villager.

Remo had had no chance. He had stood on the threshold of death. And although it went against all tradition, Chiun had inserted himself into the fight, plunging his left index nail into his first pupil's abdomen so quickly that no one saw this and Remo received credit for the victory.

"You ignore me?" Nuihc asked. "After all of these years, not even a greeting?"

"You are not real," Chiun said tightly.

Nuihc laughed. A low, heartfelt rumble that started in his bleeding belly and burst out from his pocked moon of a face. "Is this the excuse for your rudeness?" he asked. "Let me assure you then, Uncle, that I am as real as you are at this very moment. I am as real as this place of your devising, and the demons you now must face."

Chiun became slightly more interested. "You know of this place?"

Nuihc nodded. "As do you, Uncle. Here you are neither alive nor dead. Here is the 'undiscovered country' that the Englishman Shakespeare spoke of. This is the Ultimate Death. Here, your worst fears are realized." Nuihc bowed. "And I am honored to be one of your worst fears, O great Master Chiun." The arrogance of Nuihc had finally asserted itself. His face became angry. The personality change was jarring. *"You murdered me!"*

"You would have murdered my son," Chiun countered harshly, "cur of an ingrate!"

"Your 'son'!" he scoffed. "A white! Not even of the village!"

"He is more of our village than you, wicked son of my good brother!" Chiun spat.

"And is this why you killed me? For if he is truly the reason, you sullied your line for naught. He is doomed to share your fate, *gyonshi* thrall."

Chiun drew himself up haughtily, saying, "Remo will survive. He is the dead white tiger of legend. The Shiva avatar. I have seen this with my own eyes." But Nuihc had struck a nerve. There was concern in Chiun's voice. The evil Chinese bloodsuckers had decimated the House of Sinanju in times past.

Nuihc's expression became sly. "If the Master of Sinanju can be beaten by the *gyonshi*, so too can his heir," he said flatly. "As your father was bested, you were as well."

"Do not mention my father, betrayer of Sinanju!" Chiun flared. "My ears bleed, that your false tongue invokes his noble spirit."

Nuihc smiled thinly. "You accuse me of betrayal. So be it. But my treachery, as you call it, at least was known to all. Yours is far more insidious. You broke one of the most sacred tenets of the House of Sinanju to banish me here, uncle." He placed his hands on his hips. "I accuse you of treachery, Master Chiun. Your father accepted his responsibility for slaying the village elder, while you have not." Nuihc took one step back into the mist. Chiun saw that the wound in his stomach had miraculously healed. "I demand atonement for my murder!"

Chiun shook his aged head. "I will not be dictated to by a dog of your color," he hurled back. "You, who had every advantage and squandered it. You, who would take the wisdom of your ancestors and twist it to your nefarious ends. You, who scoff at every tradition you should hold most dear." But even as he spoke the words, doubts began to gather in Chiun's mind.

Nuihc's grin broadened. "I am most sorry, uncle. It is, as the French say, a *fait accompli*." He waved his hand, and the black mist seemed to appear at Chiun's feet—only this time it was not a mist but a yawning maw of a hole. And as Chiun slipped down into this funnel of inky blackness, all he could hear echoing off the endless slick walls was Nuihc's fading, taunting laughter.

The sun was setting in a dazzling reflection of orange and yellow as Remo entered the Three-G, Inc., building through a shattered window. The place seemed to be falling into disrepair.

As twilight approached, weird shadows cascaded along the gleaming hallways, sending spears of darkness along walls and into corners.

Remo wasn't sure what to expect. He didn't care.

He had only one purpose. To destroy the Leader. He was the reason all this had happened. He had engineered this entire scenario for one purpose and one purpose alone. Revenge. He had baited the trap, and Remo had willingly stepped in.

The dying sun was expending its last shred of fiery orange brilliance as Remo entered a wide reception area. A sign posted near a horseshoe-shaped desk at the center of the room read TOUR BEGINS HERE. Beyond the sign was a long hallway, off of which were dozens of closed doors.

Remo concentrated every fiber of his being on the doors in the hallway beyond. He stood stock still, his hands at his sides, as he let his mind and senses sweep down the darkening hall more effectively than any electronic sensing device.

Nothing. No movement. No breathing. There was no one in any of the offices.

Remo was about to move down the hall when he heard the first pre-attack warning noises.

And he knew he had made a cardinal mistake for someone in his profession. He had overthought his adversary. While concentrating his senses on the offices up the hallway, he had allowed his opponent to get the drop on him. Literally.

Section upon section of styrofoam ceiling panels caved in above him, showering the entrance area with a blanket of manufactured snow. Six *gyonshi* dropped from the newly made openings with surprising agility, bent at the knees, and sprang up at him. A flurry of long-nailed fingers groped for his throat.

Twisting, Remo evaded the outstretched hands and sent a fist up into the groin of the nearest man. He was rewarded with the satisfying crack of a pelvis. The man howled in pain and dropped to the floor, grabbing at his injury and accidentally stabbing himself in the thigh with his own guillotine fingernail. He howled.

On the recovering step Remo executed a backward somersault, inches ahead of the glittering ring of poisoned claws, to land on one knee on the marble-topped reception desk. He scooped up a silver letter opener and hopped lightly to the floor.

"Mail call," he told the gathering swarm.

As one, the five remaining vampires lunged. Arms slashing, teeth bared, they closed in on Remo.

"Reject meat. . . ." they chorused.

"Say no to blood," Remo shot back.

When they were an arm's length away, Remo took the blade in his teeth and grabbed the wrists of the two on the leading edge. He yanked them toward him.

Momentum carried them across the reception area.

The pair crashed through one of the huge panes of glass that made up the outer wall of the room, sending an explosion of glass out onto the well-tended front lawn of Three-G, Inc. Remo flicked a third after them. He saw with a cruel grin that one of the bodies had been impaled grotesquely on a triangular shard of glass. The point jutted through the neck of the lifeless *gyonshi*, and a film of orange smoke rose into the chilly night air. The others were already getting unsteadily to their feet, like zombies burdened with osteoporosis.

The remaining pair thrashed and lunged, desperately trying to infect Remo with their guillotine nails.

Darting under their attacks, Remo caught up their wrists and, with a jerking movement, forced their sharpened nails into one another's throats. They fell apart, going in opposite directions and surrendering a haze of orange smoke.

Remo spat the letter opener back into his hand as the two survivors he had hurled through the window clambered and stumbled back into the fray.

One was a man, the other a woman. The woman seemed unharmed, but the man, about fifty and portly, was bleeding profusely from an open head wound. He was pale and weaved unsteadily. Remo guessed he was in shock from blood loss. Assuming vampires can experience shock, that is.

The man nearly fell into Remo's arms. He tried to claw at him with his *gyonshi* fingernail, but seemed winded.

"Reject meat. . . ." he gasped. "Accept the Final Death."

"Sorry, pal," Remo said softly. "Sister Mary Margaret would never understand." With blinding swiftness, he sliced the man's throat cleanly.

The final *gyonshi* woman, in a torn black Moody Blues concert T-shirt, lunged for him. Remo simply swatted her hand down, as one might scold an angry child, and drew the letter opener across her neck.

With a shriek she floundered away, even as her gurgling throat dribbled vile orange smoke.

Six down, Remo thought. But how many more to go?

The first man Remo had felled still writhed in agony on the floor. As Remo squatted down beside him the man attempted to scratch him with his sharpened nail, while cradling his mangled lower body with his free hand.

Remo felt pity for him. Not rage, not anger. Only pity. These health-food fanatics were all pawns in a twisted demon's game of revenge. Now that Chiun was lost, it was Remo the Leader was after. And the Leader would send anyone and anything into the fray rather than face Remo himself.

After Remo had sliced the man's throat, he didn't even watch the silent plume of orange smoke. He was already walking deeper inside the Three-G building, ready for whatever horrors Sinanju's old adversary had concocted as part of his sick game of revenge.

*   *   *

He was back in Sinanju.

The main square of the village was crowded.
The villagers shouted cheers of encouragement.
The buildings were newly whitewashed. Every
nail was shiny and new. The village had never
been so neat. Even the mud flats had become a
golden beach.

Nuihc stood before him, arms crossed absently
across his chest. He wore a two-piece black
fighting outfit.

"Why have you brought me here?" Chiun
asked. He did not look at the people of Sinanju.
Their shouts were for Nuihc, not Chiun.

"It is not my doing, Uncle," Nuihc said, "but
yours."

Chiun shook his head and inhaled deeply. "It
is not I," he said.

"You," Nuihc said, smiling evilly. "And you
alone. The poison coursing through your system
has ripped away layers of your pretentious inhi-
bitions, Uncle. Is there some ghost you have yet
to exorcise?" Chiun did not respond. Nuihc's
eyes opened wide, as if suddenly alighting on a
stark truth. "Perhaps we have discovered the
one thing the infallible Chiun fears: his own un-
savory past."

Chiun brought his eyes level with Nuihc's. His
nephew's orbs burned with undisguised hatred.
Their gazes locked.

"The ignorant dog barks at its own stink," he
said, his voice dripping with contempt.

Nuihc, once Master of Sinanju, struck up a
fighting stance.

"Defend yourself, decrepit one!" he shouted.

Chiun stood his ground. "I will not fight you,
shamed one."

Nuihc's eyes became angry steel slits. "Ah, I

understand. Only when your opponent is unsuspecting, unprepared, do you strike. Here, where there are eyes to witness your treachery, you hold back. Time has addled your withered mind, uncle. You have forgotten that I do not share your compunctions. If you do not defend yourself, I will slay you like a dog in the street."

Chiun lowered his head. "So be it," he said quietly. And he turned his back in contempt.

Nuihc's eyes went wild. "I will have my revenge!"

Nuihc flew at Chiun, his index finger extended in a forward thrust—the identical stroke Chiun had landed against him years before.

Chiun would not react. He would not move to defend himself. If his physical fate was somehow sealed with his fate in this internal world of his fevered devising, then he would leave the outcome to destiny.

But he did not have the chance.

Against his will, he felt his body move. Nuihc's blow encountered vacant air as Chiun whirled, his arm swooping in a deadly arc, an out-thrust fingernail sweeping for his nephew's open chest.

At the instant the stroke should have registered, Nuihc was no longer there. In his place, several paces removed, was a man much older. He was looking at a young boy nearby. Neither had been there a moment before, Chiun was certain of that.

There was something about the older man in Nuihc's place that Chiun should have recognized, but there was no time to think. The man was stalking the boy. And his hand was streaking across the vacant space between them in molasses-slow milliseconds.

The boy! Something about the boy was familiar!

The Master of Sinanju's hand moved with the speed of a thunderbolt and the grace of a swan. He intercepted the blow. Stopped the hand. Saved the boy.

The attacking man dropped to the dust of the ground, crumpled, becoming dust himself. Chiun looked to the boy.

The boy stared back at him. He seemed fearful. Shocked. And sad. Very, very sad.

He looked up at Chiun with hauntingly familiar eyes that tore at Chiun's heart and rended his soul.

Chiun knew who the boy was. It was the young Chiun. And he had somehow become his own father.

The villagers gathered around the village elder, whom Chiun had felled. He heard their curses, felt their angry, frightened glances.

He was at once father and son. Unable to avoid destiny. Unable to evade his past.

"Murderer!" they cried.

"Betrayer!"

"You killed your own nephew, one of us!"

"Who will be next? For none of us is safe!"

And in the prison that was his mind, Chiun, Reigning Master of Sinanju, dropped to his knees and let the suppressed anguish of nearly six decades pour out onto the dusty main square of his native village.

23

The elderly Chinese known only as the Leader sat on his rude wooden throne in the security surveillance room of Three-G, Incorporated. The thick metal door was double-locked, and virtually impossible to break down with anything less than a point-blank Stinger missile strike.

A line of Sony closed-circuit television screens displayed in static-filled images the drama being played out in the complex around him.

The Leader was oblivious to the pictures on the screens. Mary Melissa Mercy was not. She continued her running narration.

"He has gotten through the first wave, Leader," she said, a twinge of nervousness in her voice.

The Leader smiled, exposing snaggly rows of stained teeth.

For this great moment, the Leader had donned a scarlet-and-gold gown over leggings and boots. A rising phoenix, its wings wide, was a stitchery of flame on his chest.

"The surprise attack failed because surprise was not on our side," he explained. "The *gweilo* knew of us. But we have not failed. We will never fail. Ours is the true faith."

Mary Melissa Mercy stared down at a TV

screen. On it, the *gweilo* Remo could be seen gliding stealthily down a corridor, away from the reception area and toward the atrium. "Will the second phase succeed?" she asked.

The Leader's smile widened until Mary Melissa could see the pits of his blackened back teeth. "With a certainty," he said. "Sinanju can be defeated by sheer numbers. This, I know. This, I know. As in Shanghai, so in this place."

His head continued to sway from side to side, as if to deny his own pronouncement.

Remo found himself in the darkened garden at the center of the Three-G complex. It was not exactly the Eden its designers had intended.

He saw dismembered bodies swinging lazily from the thickest tree branches, suspended by wire and rope. The putrid smell of rotted flesh assaulted his nostrils. The air was thick with swarms of buzzing flies.

And there were others there, as well. Hiding among the dead, pretending to be dead when they were only the undead. They had smeared one another with the blood of their victims to disguise themselves, but Remo knew they were there before they'd made their first move.

They roused, like sleepy pink bats stretching emaciated wings.

Remo deliberately had walked to the center of the garden in an attempt to appear unprepared, allowing them to surround him.

At his approach, two *gyonshi* dropped from the blackened branches of a dead oak tree like ugly fruit. One leapt over a heavy stone bench positioned at the edge of the path. A second was about to follow suit when the first rocketed backward, scooping his companion up in mid-jump.

Both slammed into the tree from which they had climbed seconds before. They became intertwined with the tree trunk. Branches fell and clattered like brittle bones.

Remo slapped imaginary dirt from his hands as a dozen more vampires closed in.

By now the moon was high above, and the approaching mob advanced with movements that suggested wolves more than men.

Their faces were pale in the reflected moonlight. Their lean shadows spread and melted together, blurring their numbers and masking their features in an on-again, off-again flicker of silvery light. A cemetery whose graves had disgorged its residents might create such a picture.

Their hands were raised in the air before them, zombie-like, as they approached with a detached animal intensity. Their eyes held the same devoid-of-thought malice displayed by Sal Mondello and the other *gyonshi*. "Reject meat. . . ." they pleaded.

"Tennis, anyone?" Remo asked coolly.

He received a chorus of hisses in reply.

"All this because my elbow was bent," Remo growled, moving into action.

He dropped back and rolled, feeling his T-shirt dampen as he encountered one of the cool, blood-seeping mounds of buried organs. He came back to his feet just beyond the reach of the vampires.

The concrete bench over which his first attackers had clambered was cool to his touch as Remo stooped and hefted it into the air, leaving twin mud furrows in the ground where it had rested.

Remo lifted the two-hundred-pound bench with no more effort than if it had been constructed of papier-mâché. He held its curved legs firmly in both hands and extended it impossibly far out in front of him, using it as a shield to ward off the blows of the deadly herd.

A twig snapped. Movement behind. There were more skulking in through the underbrush, eyes dull and feral.

A *gyonshi* nail hissed past his ear. Remo stabbed the right side of the bench outward in a sharp parry that caught the assailant in the forehead. There was a satisfying crunch of bone, and the vampire fell.

Another on his left. Two more. Both had almost landed simultaneous blows.

He stabbed out the opposite corner of the bench in rapid consecutive thrusts and the *gyonshi* fell. The rough-textured concrete was by now matted with bits of gristle and blood.

The attackers emerged from the brush. Another eight.

They merged with the original throng, venting a sort of primitive rumble of pleasure.

Remo backed against the trunk of the oak for protection.

Suddenly, a slapping hand groped from the other side. Another joined it. And another.

Balancing the bench in one hand and continuing to use it to ward off the advancing *gyonshi*, Remo shot his elbow back sharply, careful to avoid lacerating his own arm on the wicked fingernails. The unseen vampires shrieked as the bones in their hands were crushed between Remo's hammering elbow and the tree. As the collapsed appendages withdrew, three clearly defined handprints could be seen gouged in the pulpy wood.

"That's for the poisoned duck," Remo spat.

He couldn't allow himself to become careless now. He still had to find the Leader.

He pushed the heavy bench into the mob, then dropped it atop two male *gyonshis*. It burst the skull of one and crippled the second. Human brains oozed out like a fungus.

Remo bent his knees and uncoiled his legs like a spring, launching himself into the air and grabbing hold of a branch of the oak that extended out over the path. When he felt its bark almost giving way beneath his fingertips, he brought his heels against the temples of two of the vampires, breaking their necks while using them as a toehold to scramble higher into the tree.

Remo felt a slight breeze at his left calf. One of the *gyonshi* had managed to land a blow. An eight-inch gash had been slit in the back of his pant leg. It must have missed puncturing his skin by only a fraction of an inch.

They ranged below him, staring vacantly up into Remo's eyes as he crouched on the branch, considering his next move. There were too many of them to try to jump beyond them. There must have been almost thirty still standing, among them several Three-G workers whom Remo recognized. He couldn't run the risk that a *gyonshi* at the edge of the crowd might land a lucky shot as he leaped to safety.

Remo was considering other possibilities, and coming up empty, when he realized that he was not alone.

There was someone—or something—in the tree with him.

He spun on the branch, directly into the empty gaze of the late Gregory Green Gideon.

What little flesh had been left on the body was now almost completely decomposed. Gideon's eye sockets were teeming with writhing maggots. His arms and legs had been tucked away, fetal-style, inside the tree trunk with him. His splin-tery ribs reflected the white moonlight like a broken picket fence.

An idea occurred to Remo.

A few of the *gyonshi* had finally realized that they could climb up the tree after Remo. The first, the former Three-G manager named Stan, was searching out a toehold in the wide-grooved bark at the base of the tree when the first jagged rib landed.

It spiraled downward like a makeshift boomer-ang, slipping between the *gyonshi*'s own ribs and skewering his delicate heart muscle. Vampire and rib were hurled to the ground, impaled next to a mound of internal organs that had once be-longed to an organic gardener from Batavia.

"Not exactly wooden stakes, but I guess they'll do," Remo muttered. He plucked out a handful of Gideon's ribs like laths from a plaster wall, splintered the ends into rude points and let a half-dozen more fly at once.

They speared faces and necks. The gathered *gyonshi* mob screamed and howled and shrieked and fell, but not one retreated. They surged around the oak like rabid wolves, their hands raised, their fingers extended in a last desperate attempt to infect Remo with the same deadly poison that coursed through their own veins and fretted at their dead, diseased brains.

Remo threw the ribs with quick precision, until his supply ran out. There were several vampires left beneath the tree, standing among their gruesomely disfigured comrades. Remo used Gideon's shoulder blades and collar bones to finish off the last of the survivors.

When there were no *gyonshi* left standing, Remo slipped from his perch and dropped lightly to the ground.

He stood among the *gyonshi* mob, their bodies twisted, their mouths open in shock. Blood coursed from their newly formed wounds, soaking into the earth, mixing with the stagnant blood of their victims.

Remo heaved a sigh, and removed the borrowed letter opener from his back pocket. He squatted down and began the distasteful task of slitting the throats of the undead, muttering, "An assassin's work is never done."

Mary Melissa Mercy had never before seen the Leader so nervous. She had believed him to be incapable of raw fear.

Yet here he was, his head shaking determinedly from side to side, his white, unseeing eyes opened wide in his purplish face. His self-confidence seemed to be oozing out of his coarse, dead pores.

"You are fearful, O Leader?" she asked, hesitantly.

The dead face jerked up at her, his eye-slits narrowing in a mockery of sight. "All has happened as you have described it to me?" he asked, indicating the rough location of the bank of television screens.

"It has, Leader," she replied.

He set his jaw thoughtfully, and was silent for a time. Then he said, slowly, "My Creed once ruled the Asian continent, Missy. And in that time long ago, in the subcontinent now known as India, a prophesy was made. A seer who fell victim to us prophesied at the moment of his death that the second coming of the Undead would come in a land yet unknown. And in that land, the last *gyonshi* would tremble at the sound of the voice of a god who was not the one God." His voice trailed off.

Mary Melissa shook her head. "There is only one God," she said with certainty. "The God of our Creed, who bids us to punish the stomach-desecrators."

The Leader's dead face sank, as the brain within his skull succumbed to dark thoughts. "This is the second time I have visited the Final Death on this land, and this is the second time I have faced the *gweilo* of the Sinanju Master."

Mary Melissa's brow furrowed. "What would you have us do, Leader?"

"Fight to the death, Missy. It is all we can do." His jaw snapped shut like a bony vise, and his thin lips pressed tightly together.

The production floor of Three-G, Inc., was silent as a tomb. Moonlight filtered through the ceiling-to-floor windows, throwing a ghostly semi-light over the huge room.

Remo left the door behind him open, as he padded quietly across the concrete floor toward the nearest metal staircase. He glanced up at the X-shaped catwalk that connected all four corners of the second-story level. He saw no one through the tiny diamond shapes that the catwalk flooring formed.

He was slipping past the dormant conveyor belt when he saw a figure hiding in its shadow. It was definitely female.

Remo recognized her from his last trip to Three-G: Elvira McGlone. He cleared his throat by way of warning.

She spun around to face him. Even in shadow,

her eyes were desperate and fearful, like those
of a rabbit transfixed by the headlights of a car.
Her face might have been enmeshed in the hypo-
thetical car's grille.

"Miss McCrone?" Remo asked. Her fingernails, including her index finger, were still coated
in the same bloodred polish. She was not *gyonshi*.
He was sure of it. Her index fingernails tapered
to points, not edges.

"McGlone," she corrected. With one hand,
she attempted to adjust the lines on her tattered
skirt as she rose to face Remo. She pretended
nonchalance, while her body language screamed
her fear.

"Sorry," Remo said, taking a step toward her.

"Don't come any closer!" Elvira McGlone
hissed. Even before she wheeled on him, Remo
knew that she was shielding a revolver in her
other hand. "I swear I'll blow your brains out!"
She waggled the weapon menacingly.

"No bullets," Remo said, nodding toward the
revolver, whose exposed cylinder chambers were
like tiny caverns. It might as well have been a
pencil sharpener. He glanced around the production room disinterestedly. He wondered if there
were more vampires hiding close by. Waiting to
pounce.

"Don't test me," Elvira McGlone said. The
gun-waggling had become more pronounced.

"And don't kid me," Remo returned, reaching
over to pluck the weapon from her hand. He
flipped open the cylinder and shook it like a salt-
shaker. Nothing came out. "See? Empty." He
tossed the gun away.

Elvira McGlone started backing away, like a
toy doll whose batteries have been inserted
upside-down. She whipped two Waterman pens

from a pocket of her mannish tailored suit and crossed them protectively before her.

"You keep away!" she shrieked, pushing back into the conveyor belt. In her haste, she tripped over a plastic rubbish barrel and landed on her best side. Her backside. One of the pens rolled away out of sight.

"Don't sweat it," said Remo, who, until this last manifestation of fright, had thought she couldn't possibly become any more repulsive. "I'm not one of them."

"I don't care! Go away!" she said, groping her way to her feet.

Remo reached down and took Elvira McGlone by the back of the neck. He hauled her to her feet, working her neck vertebrae with hard fingers until her body relaxed to nearly its normal level of tension.

The fear drained from her eyes.

"Let's have it," Remo urged.

"They've been stalking me for days," she said, catching her breath. "I don't dare trust anyone."

"Check out the fingernails," Remo said. He offered his hands to her, nail-side up.

She studied them cautiously, her breathing still heavy. "Okay," she said uncertainly. "Maybe you are normal."

"If I wasn't, you'd be one of them by now," Remo pointed out.

"Okay, okay. You've sold me. Just what the hell is going on here?" she demanded, her voice a hoarse whisper. She peered over the top of the conveyor belt behind her.

"Would you believe me if I told you we're surrounded by vampires?" he asked.

She shook her head. "A week ago, I would have thought you were as flaky as everyone else around here. But now . . ." she composed herself. "I walked in on them while they were turning some of the tourists Gideon brings through here into human slumgullion. That Mercy woman was at the center of it all. When she saw me, I ran. I've tried to get out, but they're watching all the doors. I've kept out of sight, changing hiding places when I can to fool them."

"They're not very bright," Remo pointed out.

Elvira McGlone nodded her head toward where her pistol had skittered away in the shadows.

"But they're dangerous," she said wryly, "and you just tossed away our only protection."

"It was empty," Remo said, moving toward the stairs.

"That's because I took out six of them the first day," she explained. When he glanced back at her, she shrugged and added, "I worked five years in a New York ad agency." She followed him cautiously. "My survival skills are as sharp as a U.S. Ranger's."

Remo hadn't gone up four steps before he spotted a small dark figure hiding behind one of the upright metal banisters. It was the emaciated tiger-stripe cat he had seen during his tour of the Three-G plant with Mary Melissa Mercy.

It cringed in the darkness, its back arched, its mangy fur slowly rising like porcupine quills.

Remo reached out to the creature. "You tried to warn me about her, didn't you, tiger?" he said gently.

There was a gleam in the reflected moonlight. Something was wrong. It was the look in the animal's eyes. It was the same dead-eyed stare he had been given by his *gyonshi* attackers.

The cat hissed and spat at Remo, lashing out with its poisoned claws.

Remo allowed the animal to bound away. It flew backward off the staircase and into the production area, landing roughly against an opened electrical panel.

The panel sparked at the cat's impact, casting a bright blue aura over the four enormous stainless-steel cauldrons on the main floor.

The cat dropped to the floor, severely singed but alive. It struggled, finally found its paws, and limped off into the darkness.

Remo could smell burnt fur. But there was something else. The orange smoke. Very faint. Not quite as much as from a human host. It dribbled up from the cat's tiny nostrils.

The thin cloud rose eerily in the moonlight, then dissipated.

Remo nodded his head in silent understanding as he mounted the stairs double-time. Elvira followed.

They found themselves alone on the second level, overlooking the main production floor. The catwalk extended before and behind them into the shadows.

"An old Chinese man," Remo said, turning to Elvira McGlone. "Have you seen him?"

"Yes," she replied. "He spends most of his time with that Mercy ghoul. I think they're in the security room." She leveled a bloodred fingernail and added, "The metal door at the far end of the walkway."

"Thanks. Now go back to the spot where we met until I come back for you." Remo was just about to move down the catwalk when Elvira spoke, her voice low and husky.

"There's one more thing."

"What?" Remo said distractedly, hesitating.

"This." With a flick of her thumb the artificial

nail popped off her index finger, revealing the chopped-off *gyonshi* guillotine edge. Before the red crescent press-on nail hit the floor, Elvira McGlone had slashed her hand in a perfect diagonal, opening Remo's shirt from shoulder to stomach.

Eyes wide, Remo jumped back, only to find himself pinned against the railing, the production floor below him. He looked down at himself. No blood. She hadn't broken the skin. Elvira slashed out again. Remo leaned back farther, ready to grab her wrist as she withdrew. He never got the chance.

The metal railing creaked and gave way. Too late, Remo noticed the shiny bright slits that the hacksaw had made at either end of the railing section. He toppled over backward and plunged toward a huge stainless-steel cauldron far below that was filled with shadows—and who knew what else.

His mind exploded with a sudden grisly recollection.

Didn't the *gyonshi* also boil their victim's blood in big pots before drinking it?

24

At Folcroft Sanitarium, Dr. Lance Drew was losing a patient.

"He isn't responding!" The replacement nurse's voice was full of tension and frustration. The heart monitor, which had been beeping like a video game with a nine-year-old Nintendo master at the controls, went quiet.

"Pressure's bottomed out. He's arrested!"

Dr. Drew grabbed the twin paddles from the portable heart unit next to the bed. "Clear!" he ordered. Beads of perspiration had formed on his forehead. As one, the medical team jumped back from the bed. The doctor placed the paddles on the pale, thin chest and shocked the heart muscle. He looked up expectantly at the monitor. Still flat-lined.

"Nothing," said the second doctor.

Dr. Drew clenched his jaw determinedly. "Clear!" he commanded again. He shocked the heart a second time.

There was an echoing blip on the nearby monitor. Another. It was followed by a string of beeps.

"Pulse is climbing!" called the nurse. "Heart rate increasing!"

The body on the bed arched its back as if in pain, and began spewing a thin cloud of saffron smoke from its mouth and nose.

"My God, what is *that*?" the nurse asked, incredulous.

Dr. Drew gripped the paddles more tightly. He stared at the orange smoke as it rose in the air, spread across the acoustical ceiling tiles, and faded in the glow of the fluorescent light. He shook his head in awe.

The second doctor looked up from the monitoring equipment. It was beeping steadily now. "Heart rate's back to normal," he breathed. He glanced toward the others, a look of intense relief on his young face. "He's out of it."

All those in the room released their breaths—for the first time realizing they had been holding them.

The team became engrossed with their patient once more, forgetting, for the moment, the strange phenomenon they had just witnessed.

On the bed, Dr. Harold W. Smith's face relaxed, seeming more at peace than it had been in many years.

25

The first danger, Remo knew, was the falling railing. It was sharp at both ends. Sharp enough to impale him if he fell on it.

Remo slipped his fingers around the railing and, using his waist as leverage for his arms, twisted in midair to flick the heavy length of steel a safe distance away.

He relaxed his muscles, and tucked his legs in close to his body in order to avoid any broken bones.

And so fell neatly into one of the giant stainless-steel cauldrons.

Remo landed on his feet, in darkness. The big object was empty. No blood. No floating bone or human matter. Just slick, shiny steel all around him.

Too slick and shiny to climb. Remo prepared to run up one side, knowing that once momentum enabled him to reach the lip he could launch himself back up onto the catwalk.

He was preparing to do just that when the production facility sprang noisily to life.

All over the floor, lights lit and machinery began to roar at an ear-pounding volume.

The floor of the tureen Remo stood upon began

a relentless move inward on itself, spiraling toward a trio of narrow holes at its center. Razor-sharp stainless-steel blades pounded into view above the holes.

Obviously they had been designed to chop up something, probably an ingredient for one of Three-G's many health products, and funnel the residue down the production line. Remo was determined not to become one of those ingredients.

He hit the spinning metal floor on his feet and leapt out of the deadly trap. At the same moment, a mass of hard-shelled walnuts was released from a storage bin directly above the tureen.

They struck Remo like a dense, crunchy water-fall and carried him back inside the cauldron, where the deadly blades continued to whir remorselessly.

He slid on the floor, feeling the inexorable drag toward its center. He pulled himself to his feet with difficulty. The undulating sea of brown walnuts had buried him to the chest. He could feel the vibrations of the shells as they were crushed beneath his feet.

The jump would be more difficult now. The sound of whirring Servo-Motors came from somewhere in the ceiling high above. He tried to steady himself but felt his legs gliding slowly inward, like water to a drain.

The whirring sound above him abruptly stopped.

Remo did not even have a chance to push off the floor when the second mass of walnuts fell. For a second he scrambled amid them like a drowning man, but the pull from below was too great.

As the machinery continued to rumble its cacophony of death, Remo allowed himself to be dragged to the tureen bottom.

One hand shot up, like that of a drowning man, only to sink back beneath the crunchy morass.

Elvira McGlone released the controls, turned to the nearest TV monitor, and gave a thumbs-up sign. Her eyes were dead.

Mary Melissa Mercy smiled tightly. "The *gweilo* is no more Leader," she announced.

The Leader leaned forward, the swaying motion of his head lessening as his expression tightened. "You see his body, Missy?" he asked, a trace of eagerness adding an edge to the rasp that was his voice.

Mary Melissa Mercy peered more closely at the television monitor. The noise from the production floor poured out of a tinny speaker at the end of the console. All she could make out in the fuzzy black-and-white image was the shifting pile of walnuts. There was no sign of the *gweilo*, Remo. "He has vanished below the surface, Master. But no one could survive the chopping blades of that machine. Not even one of these impure Sinanju duck-eaters."

The Leader slumped back in his chair, tired from all his efforts. "My soul rejoices," he said, nodding. "If a carcass should surface, prepare it in the prescribed manner of my ancestors."

"Yes, Leader."

He listened as she left the room. He heard the locks of the heavy metal door clanging back into place as she closed it behind her.

The girl was happy once more. He could tell by the light tread of her heavy shoes. She had become concerned momentarily, but that concern had vanished along with the *gweilo*. She had reverted back to her innate self-confidence.

The Leader was pleased, as well. His Creed had survived its greatest challenge. He could now fulfill his destiny. The Final Death would now be achieved without interference.

The sounds from the production floor continued to squawk from the small speaker. The Leader was half listening to them when he heard another sound.

A new sound. Different from the rest. It was a sort of wrenching whine, like that of complicated machinery being forced to run backward by a force stronger still. It was succeeded by a rumbling hiss.

The Leader did not hear the three consecutive pops as the blades at the base of the tureen were snapped loose. Nor did he hear the grinding protest as they were wedged back into the mechanism to stop the motion of the floor.

The wrenching sound he did hear was that of the stainless-steel tureen into which the walnuts had been poured. Two hand prints had appeared on its smooth outer surface and were gliding downward, as if the steel were rubber. Ten-finger furrows marred the shiny texture. Halfway down the hand marks separated, tearing a gouge from the top of the tureen to its base as easily as if it were paper.

The screech of metal was unearthly.

The rumbling hiss that had accompanied the sound of the tureen's destruction was that of the walnuts spilling out across the production room floor.

After the noises had died down and the last lonely nut had rolled to a stop, the Leader remained puzzled.

He could not see Remo stepping through the opening, his eyes dead, black pools of menace. He did not see Remo flicking one of the walnuts upward to the catwalk, knocking Elvira McGlone unconscious. He knew only that the feeling of cold dread from before had returned.

A hollow voice boomed out, crystal-clear over the static of the speaker, louder than the loudest machinery.

And the hollow voice intoned: *"I am created Shiva, the Destroyer; death, the shatterer of worlds. The dead night tiger made whole by the Master of Sinanju. Who is this dog meat that dares challenge me?"*

Feeling his thin blood turning to ice, the Leader of the *gyonshi* trembled uncontrollably.

Remo Williams mounted the stairs in a single leap. Elvira McGlone was sprawled across the catwalk. He'd take care of her later.

Remo slid past her and moved swiftly along the walkway.

Someone stood at the far end. In the shadows. Mary Melissa Mercy. His final obstacle.

"You just don't know when to quit, do you, duck-eater?" Mary Melissa taunted, her naked green eyes blazing.

"Big talk, coming from a cannibal," Remo returned.

He continued moving toward her.

"We only drink blood. And you have no idea what you're dealing with," she warned. She found that she did not have to force confidence into her voice. "We possess powers no meat-eater can understand."

Remo remained silent.

"Your old friend understands now," she said,

hoping to elicit a reaction. None came. "I am one with the Leader. The others you have defeated were nothing. Mere agents of our Creed. The old Korean knew that." She took a step toward him, still in shadow. "If the Master of Sinanju can be defeated, why not his pupil?"

Remo continued to move silently toward her across the raised platform.

Any hesitation Mary Melissa Mercy had felt before was gone. Her adrenaline flow continued in its wild rise. Her heart rate was more than double what it would have been had not the *gyonshi* infection empowered her purified blood.

"My Leader tells me that your Sinanju is a powerful force," she said. "But I've learned to master the secrets of something far more potent." She spread her hands like a game show hostess. "Behold!"

A dark mist seeped up and around the body of Mary Melissa Mercy. In an instant, she was enveloped in a sepia pall.

Remo, whose eyes ordinarily could break down fog or smoke into its component molecules, and see beyond as if it were only a light haze, could make out no shape within the inky blackness.

This was it. The infamous *gyonshi* mist Chiun had warned him about. Well, Remo had his trump card. He would not invite Mary Melissa Mercy in. He just hoped she was a stickler for tradition.

Cautiously, he pressed against the railing. He noticed it too had been hacksawed into a subtle trap. No doubt there were other traps about.

The mist spread slowly and insidiously along the length of the catwalk, until it was only a breath away from Remo.

There was something odd. The clank of footfalls on the metal catwalk. Should that have been there?

A long-nailed hand slashed out from within the dense black mist.

Remo shrank back. Just in time. The hand whizzed past his face and disappeared back inside the fog.

If a vampire can actually become mist, Remo wondered, will it still make audible footfalls? He decided to test his theory.

The hand slashed out again. Remo wrapped his fingers around the delicate wrist and tugged. Mary Melissa Mercy reappeared more easily than she had vanished. Although much less daintily. She did a half-flip through the air and landed roughly on her backside in the center of the walkway.

The black mist continued to billow and hiss behind Remo. A break in the cloud showed the stuff pouring from a metal grate at the base of the wall. "Thought so," he said, nodding to himself.

Confidently, his face a gigantic cruel smile, he advanced on Mary Melissa Mercy.

She had crawled back to her feet, and was in a sort of half-crouch as Remo approached. She brandished her *gyonshi* finger before her like a stiletto.

"Stay back!" she warned, slashing the air between them.

"Try garlic," Remo taunted. "Or am I thinking of werewolves?"

He grabbed her wrist firmly in his hand, being careful to keep the *gyonshi* fingernail at a safe distance, then bent Mary Melissa Mercy onto his hip. As he carried her down the stairs to the production floor she made repeated attempts to

bite his arm and to claw him with her free hand,
but he ignored those futile gestures.

After a short search Remo found an open electrical panel. He lifted Mary Melissa to it, careful
to keep her right hand pinned to her side. She
thrashed and screeched, but Remo's grip was
firmer than iron.

With his other hand, he unscrewed the glass
fuses.

Slowly, Remo bent her face into the exposed
contacts. He growled, "Kiss this," gave her a
hard push and retreated.

A violent hiss of blue sparks resulted.

The light show lasted only for a moment. Mary
Melissa, limbs quivering, sprang away from the
panel and fell heavily to the floor.

Remo watched with interest as Mary Melissa
Mercy struggled to her knees. When she lifted
her dazed face to his own, he nearly let out a
whoop of triumph.

Her fiery red hair smoked at the ends. But that
was not all that rose from Mary Melissa Mercy.
The orange fog was pouring out of her mouth
and nose.

"No!" she screamed thinly, clawing at the eva-
sive vapor. "Noooo!"

Like some possessed ex-smoker, she scrambled
after the cloud as it rose, frantically trying to
draw it back inside her lungs.

"You know what they say about secondhand
smoke," Remo warned. "It's a killer."

But Mary Melissa paid his taunt no heed. She
was on her tiptoes moments after the smoke had
vanished, still gulping at the air frantically.
Nothing happened. She dropped back to the
balls of her feet and her eyes careened wildly
around the room, as if desperate for a fix.

She looked down at her hand. And seemed to hit upon an idea.

Mary Melissa Mercy began stabbing at her own throat, attempting to reinfect herself with her *gyonshi* fingernail. She succeeded only in opening her carotid artery. Blood spurted out with each of her still rapid heartbeats, pooling on the cold concrete floor. Dazed, Mary Melissa Mercy fell back to her knees. She looked up imploringly at Remo, who regarded her with cold, unsympathetic eyes.

"The Leader . . ." she gasped. "The Leader . . . can save me."

Remo shook his head. "Not where he's going," he said solemnly.

The machines had ceased their merciless thrumming.

The Leader did not notice. His mind was locked on one thing and one thing alone: the Final Death. The contagion that would erase the stomach-desecrators and restore purity to the once clean face of the impure earth.

He did not hear Mary Melissa Mercy cry out as Remo delivered a killing blow. He did not see him move along the catwalk.

Only when the thick metal door to the security room burst inward with a crash did he know the *gweilo* had found him.

His face jerked toward the distraction, his blind eyes like nystagmic pinballs.

"Sinanju . . ." he whispered vacantly. His shoulders collapsed.

"We have unfinished business," he heard the voice of the *gweilo* say.

"I, too, had a mission," he rasped. "You have prevented me from fulfilling this sacred duty."

"That's the biz, sweetheart," the *gweilo* called Remo said.

The Leader's white eyes flew open in sudden remembrance. His lips formed a gleeful leer. "We have the soul of your master!" he cried victoriously. "He writhes in the Ultimate Death, and so is lost to you forever!"

"Forever is a whisper in the Void to Sinanju," returned Remo.

The Leader's shoulder's sagged, like a slowly bending wire hanger. The *gweilo* had seemed indifferent to his boast. "You do not understand!" he spat.

"Wrong," Remo said coldly. "I understand perfectly. I can't undo the past. But I can avoid the mistakes of the past. And you represent a big one."

The Leader's voice became the hiss of an angry serpent. "My Creed is as old as time! We are older than your pathetic House!"

Remo shrugged. "We've all got to go sometime."

He advanced on the Leader.

And in the eternal blackness in which he dwelt, the Leader saw something he had not witnessed in generations.

Color.

And the color was the hue of blood.

Somehow, it was inside both of his eyes.

Then it was gone.

And so was he.

26

Chiun walked alone in the hills east of Sinanju.

The evergreen trees pointed toward the heavens, some so high that they seemed to yearn for the clouds gathered above. Shafts of bright amber sunlight raked the sky like hollow swords. The air was cold and clean.

He walked the brown earth, between sharp inclines covered in rich green.

There was someone waiting for him up ahead, where the path diverged. Chiun knew he would be waiting here. Just as he had been waiting for him for nearly five decades.

The tall man wore a white shirt with a tight waist and loose sleeves, a pair of baggy black pants that tightened at the ankles, white leggings, and black sandals. His hair was short and black, his features were proud. His eyes were the shape of almonds and the color of steel.

The man smiled warmly at Chiun's approach.

"Hello, Father," Chiun said.

"My son," said the tall, handsome man. He looked Chiun up and down, nodding his approval. "You have grown," he said. He had not aged a day since Chiun had last seen him.

"It has been many years, Father."

243

"Yes. Yes, I suppose it has." There was a hint of sadness in his strong voice.

An awkward silence hung between the two—together as men for the first time.

"Why are you here, Chiun the Younger?" his father asked at last.

"I am young no longer, Father," Chiun explained. "I ceased to be young both in name and in spirit on the day you went into the hills. Little did I know then that my burdens were just beginning."

"And your pupil?"

"Alas, the son of my brother turned his back on our village," he said sadly. "I was forced to deal with him severely."

"Our disgrace is the same," Chiun the Elder said, nodding. "Mine public, yours private." He smiled. "To me you will always be 'young Chiun,' my son."

Young Chiun's wispy beard trembled. "You know of my crime, father?"

"Not a crime. A necessity. The boy was a renegade who had to be brought to task. No one but you could have fulfilled this duty. Your son in Sinanju was saved. The line will continue." He paused. "How is he, by the way?"

"Remo?" Chiun asked. "I know not, Father."

His father's eyes grew moist. "My grandson in Sinanju," he said wistfully.

"Remo is a fine boy, Father," Chiun agreed. "Pigheaded at times, but he respects our history. His history."

"Just as we have respected that same history?" Chiun the Elder laughed. "We are the same, you and I," he said, staring absently at a cleft in the wall of rock beyond.

Chiun knew where his father's thoughts were

drifting. "You did only what you had to do, Father," he told the man who was now, inexplicably, younger than himself.

"As did you, Son. Why do you torment yourself?"

"My ancestors were shamed by my deed," Chiun said, his head bowed.

Chiun the Elder spread generous arms. "I am not ashamed. Am I not your most cherished ancestor?"

"You do not understand," Chiun said, his wrinkled face still downcast.

Chiun the Elder extended one hand, raising his son's chin until their eyes locked. "Know you this, my son. I understand more than any other. You think you have performed the most despicable of deeds. But it is only so here." He placed his fingertips against Chiun's forehead. "You know in your heart that the act you were forced to perform was just and right. As do I. You will never have peace nor leave this place until you come to understand that the greatest battle a man can win is the one within himself."

Old Chiun the Younger remained silent, contemplating his father's words.

"How is it you come to be here?" the old-man-who-was-young asked finally.

"I was protecting the boy, Father. My son is very strong in body, but not yet powerful enough in mind. Had he been banished to this place he would have built a home, married an angel, and fathered strapping boys with properly shaped eyes. He still yearns for peace, and the things he cannot have. He accepts what he should not and does not accept what he should." Chiun's words were more for himself than anyone else.

"Like you, my son?"

Chiun seemed uncertain. "Perhaps."

The handsome young old man clasped his hands behind his back. "We sacrifice for our children," he said simply. "It is the most difficult duty we are called upon to perform. And the most noble. Fortunate are those who are called to the temple of fatherhood."

Chiun's hazel eyes glistened in the starlight. "I missed you, Father."

Chiun the Elder smiled. "Yes, my son. I know. Your devotion sustained me in my last days in these mountains. When I looked to the sky, I saw you. The eternity of nothingness was filled by you." He shook his head. "For me there was no emptiness, no suffering. I survived in you. And in your promise."

Chiun looked into the eyes of the man who had taught him so much in so precious little time. "I loved you, Father," he whispered. "I have abandoned mercy, pity, remorse, but I do know love. That was your greatest gift to me. Thank you, Father. Thank you."

The handsome visage of Chiun the Elder turned to his son, and his smile lit the heavens. Then he became the heavens, his face turning into the sky and stars.

Chiun looked up at the night, which now hemmed in the mountains, and felt all eternity around him. But it was no longer cold and distant.

At last, he understood.

The Leader had opened the recesses of Chiun's mind with his *gyonshi* poison. It was no wonder that no one returned after glimpsing this. Their bodies were merely empty shells for the poison that raged in their systems, driving the victim to attack without conscience or compunction. Their minds lived on in the hell or paradise of their own imaginings.

To remain was tempting. Here, anything was possible.

Chiun heaved a sigh and turned his back on eternity. There was still much he had to do. The work on Remo's body was all but finished. It could hardly grow any more skillful. But there was much yet to be done with the potentially limitless power of his mind.

"Sinanju swine!"

Chiun spun when he heard the taunt in Korean. "Who dares call me thus?" he shouted. The darkness had become total, bathing the mountains until they were immersed in a sea of sludge.

There was something about the darkness. Something vague. Something . . . inviting.

"I dare, puny one! Prepare yourself!"

The voice was getting closer. Chiun spun in the opposite direction. "Show yourself!" he demanded. He expected to see Nuihc once more, returned to goad him into battle. Instead, the figure that seemed to step through a slice in the darkness was wrinkled, small, and dressed in a mandarin's robe. He had a fringe of steel-blue hair, like a metallic halo that had fallen, and his skin was the color of a Concord grape.

The Leader. His pearl eyes burned with a chill fire.

"We meet again, Korean," he rasped.

The blackness of the sky was forming a pool on the ground nearby. Something was drawing Chiun toward the orifice.

"Begone, vision!" he commanded. "I am leaving this place. Do not dare attempt to prevent me."

The Leader merely leered. "You will never leave this place."

Chiun met the leer with a confident smile. "I will—now that you are here to take my place."

The Leader flew at him. Chiun struck a defensive posture. They collided, twin furies unleashed.

The fight was extraordinary, impossible, titanic. The heavens cracked with the sound of mighty blows. Five thousand years of history flowed perfectly and precisely together from their limbs. They danced with death, every muscle coming into play, the neurons of their brains sparking like flashbulbs.

Their fingers, palms, wrists, forearms, elbows, upper arms, shoulders, necks, chins, heads, torsos, waists, hips, thighs, knees, calves, feet and toes intermingled, striking and blocking at the same time—each thrust countered like two faucets of water opened full, melding together in one fantastic waterfall.

They fought furiously in the space of their two bodies, their arms making intricate patterns and their legs swinging up, around, in front, to the side, and behind, as if attached to their pelvis by rubber bands. They spun in space, their fists striking each other in furious rhythm, always connecting with impotent blows.

Neither won, but neither lost. They mirrored each other, clashing in perfect harmony. Their blows became faster and faster and faster still, until everything in their heads became a blur. The sound of their movements buzzed, interrupted only by the continual, closely-spaced slaps of contact. Their fight became a strange, aching song of violence.

"Live!" a voice boomed in Chiun's head. It

was deafening, but Chiun had no time to pay it heed.

The battle continued.

"Live!" the voice commanded again. It seemed somehow familiar. "I was poisoned years ago. I was unconscious. Near death. You thought I didn't hear you, but I did. Live!" ordered the voice, which was no longer unfamiliar. "It is all you told me, it is all I tell you. You cannot die unless you will it, and I will not allow it. I need you."

Chiun had no choice but to ignore the voice. The battle still raged. He could not pause, lest he be slain.

They would have fought forever if Remo had not appeared above them. He dropped toward them, ready to strike. He wore the black, beltless two-piece fighting garment of the traditional Sinanju pupil.

"Remo!" Chiun cried. "My son! No! Leave this place!"

"Kill him, *gweilo!*" the Leader shouted. "You are heir to Sinanju! Do as your destiny commands!"

Remo smiled, his expression deadly, raising his hand as he prepared to cleave one of the combatants in half.

For one horrible instant, the Master of Sinanju believed that his worst nightmares were about to come true. Feared that Remo did indeed seek his throne, his treasure, his honor. He had never believed it before. The charge was just his way to compel obedience in the wayward white.

Then Remo fell upon the fear-struck Leader, crushing him to nothingness and disappearing into the pool of blackness that endlessly spilled from the heavens.

For a moment Chiun stood alone in eternity, his breathing difficult, his chest aching.

"I'm not going to wait all day, Little Father," Remo's voice whispered in his ear.

A sensation of warmth spread up from the pit of the Master of Sinanju's stomach. It radiated outward across his torso, seeking his heart. The pit of the Oriental soul met and joined forces with the Occidental seat of love.

For an instant Chiun was a young man again—standing at the edge of his village with the voices of celebration behind him, his father's back vanishing into the mountains before him.

But he no longer felt the same isolation. The same feeling of loss.

The Master of Sinanju looked up at the heavens, put his feet together, and took a small hop. He disappeared into the inky blackness.

27

Chiun's old, old eyes fluttered open.

Remo stood beside his bed, two strange paddles in his hands. He hooked the paddles into two slots on the side of an upright wheeled cart.

"How are you feeling?" Remo asked. His voice was filled with concern, but his face beamed with joy.

Chiun saw the ghostly image of the orange *gyonshi* mist thinning and spreading along the ceiling. "The bad air is no more?" he said wonderingly.

Smith lay on the bed across the room. He had turned so as to look at Remo and Chiun. His eyes were rimmed in black, his skin a paler gray than normal. Most would have smiled at Chiun in encouragement, but Smith managed only a formal bow of the head. "Master of Sinanju," he croaked.

"Emperor Smith," Chiun said, returning Smith's gesture with a barely visible nod. "I trust you are well."

"I seem to have suffered a heart attack," Smith returned weakly. "But I am on the mend, the doctor says, thanks to a timely electrical re-stimulation of the muscle."

"You have the heart of a lion," Chiun said loud enough for all to hear. "Let no one doubt this." Then, beckoning for Remo to come closer, he lifted his head slightly.

Remo leaned over the bed, tipping his ear close to Chiun's mouth. "Yes, Little Father?" he asked.

"Be a good boy, and see that I get a private room."

Two weeks passed before Remo and Chiun were able to return to the Catskill Mountains.

The press had long since departed, explaining away the deaths at Poulette Farms as an unusually severe political statement by some concerned but nutritionally unbalanced vegetarians, out to avenge the food-poisoning epidemic that the USDA had officially traced to Poulette Farms and only Poulette Farms.

Henry Cackleberry Poulette had been officially blamed for the epidemic. His personal psychiatrist had held a press conference, explaining his late patient's pathological hatred of chickens.

Within the hour, he was fielding multimillion dollar offers for transcripts of his private sessions with the Chicken King.

Smith had had the *gyonshi* victims at Three-G carted away in secret. Remo didn't ask how. He didn't care. Smith had told him that so many bloodless, butchered bodies would be difficult to explain away. Let the world simply think the vengeful Vegans had closed up shop after visiting justice on Henry Poulette.

Remo and Chiun climbed the mountain above Poulette Farms, and it was several minutes before they exchanged a word. They moved in harmonious unison, letting the warmth of the spring afternoon wash over them in cleansing waves.

It was a gorgeous day. The sun shone brightly through the swaying branches and broad green leaves. Fragrant blossoms mingled their scents in the air.

"How did you know that the *gyonshi* virus could be purged by electricity?" Chiun finally asked.

"A cat told me," Remo said nonchalantly.

Chiun nodded in satisfaction. "Cats are very wise, my son," he said. "Although sons are wiser at times." His eyes shone as they gazed upon his pupil.

Remo offered a small bow of his head.

They were silent yet again.

That was all Chiun had needed, during his titanic struggle with the Leader, to tip the odds in his favor. The knowledge that Remo was there for him when he needed him most. He had manifested Remo into a physical presence in his mind, allowing him to defeat the forces that trapped him. Those forces being his own poisoned neural system.

"The *gyonshi*?" He had not asked about them during the two weeks of recuperation at Folcroft. Even now the question seemed superfluous.

"A sham," said Remo. "Whatever they once were was long gone. The only thing they had left was the virus. Everything else was a pale plagiarism of their ancestors' legends. The mist. The blood-drinking. Everything."

They climbed the hill parallel to each other, walking some ten feet apart. The grass sprang immediately back to life after they had passed, as if only wind, not human feet, had pressed it down.

The ultramodern Three-G building leaped into view as they passed through a thicket of shrubs at the top of the mountain.

They had finally reached the summit, and now stood where the luxurious garden at the center of the building stretched out into the surrounding countryside.

Turning, they looked down on the valley below, neither bothering to squint in the glorious sunlight which bathed them.

"And the Leader?" Chiun asked, not looking at Remo.

Remo seemed disinterested. He raised his head a centimeter.

Chiun did not have to look up, but he did. In the tallest part of the rotted oak tree which squatted at the center of the garden, hung a skeleton. Its flesh had been completely shorn from muscles. Its muscles and tendons were completely ripped from its bones. Its bones were white and gleaming, as if they had been shined to a perfect luster. Its eyes rested, unstalked, inside its open eye sockets. Every other tooth had been surgically removed.

It smiled a checkerboard smile, its pupils cockeyed.

Remo entered the grove. Chiun followed in silence.

The bodies of the vampires were gone. Everything was as it had been the first time Chiun had entered the large garden, save for one detail.

With his toe, Chiun touched the earth by the base of the oak tree. It was soggy with blood. Beneath a thin cover of dirt the internal organs rested—crushed to plasmic puddles, then wrapped and knotted inside the Chinese's own pale purple skin.

Remo had been very busy during Chiun's recuperation. Even now he seemed preoccupied. Remo reached inside a large, open knothole in the side of the tree and removed a whole, perfectly preserved brain. He placed it at his teacher's sandaled feet.

"This time," the future Master of Sinanju said, straightening. "I positively, definitely, absolutely, without a doubt, did not bend my elbow."

The present Master of Sinanju smiled with pride upon his student, then brought his foot down in the exact center of the dead, gray mass.